P9-EED-303

MATCH POINT

DORI'S BIG MOMENT

The long, hard hours of grueling practice . . . the tension, thrills, and heartbreaks of the tournament trail . . . the struggle to control her own fiery temper—none of it had been easy for Dori Sinclair. But her drive to become a tennis champion had kept her going, even after her greatest disappointments.

Now it was the biggest moment of her young life, the climax of her tennis career. She faced her arch-rival, knowing that if she won this point, she would win the national championship. . . .

Could she do it? Or would Dori Sinclair again be a runner-up?

MATCH POINT

By Owenita Sanderlin

Illustrated by Marilyn Hamann

Cover by Ben Otero

GOLDEN PRESS
Western Publishing Company, Inc.
Racine, Wisconsin

©1979 by Western Publishing Company, Inc.
All rights reserved. Produced in U.S.A.

GOLDEN® and GOLDEN PRESS® are trademarks
of Western Publishing Company, Inc.

No part of this book may be reproduced or
copied in any form without written permission
from the publisher.

0-307-21518-0

Dedicated to
Kathy, Teri, Stevie. Bryan, Craig, Christy,
Paul, Wendy, John, Michelle, Kevin,
Lori, and Debbie

CONTENTS

PART ONE

1 • WORLD'S WORST BABY-SITTER

My sister Stacy is sixteen. She's The Oldest. Davy is fifteen. He's The Boy. Betsy is The Baby, even though she's six now and going on seven. All I am is Twelve. It sure is hard to get noticed when you're nothing special, but I manage.

"Dori, pick your things up," Mom says about ten times a day.

"Dori! Turn down that stereo," Dad is always yelling.

And I have to baby-sit Betsy all the time while Stacy and Davy get to be tennis champions.

I wish *I* could play tennis. Like this week, at La

Jolla (which you're supposed to pronounce La HOY-yah), they're having the big tournament they have every July, and people come from all over California and even from other states to play in it. We only have to drive twenty miles from where we live in the back-country.

They have divisions in both singles and doubles—that's when you play with a partner—for everybody in the family. Mostly my family play singles. Grand-ma is in the Senior Women's (old ladies'). Dad is in the Junior Veterans', which means he's over thirty-five. Stacy's playing in the Girls' Eighteen and Under, Davy's in the Boys' Sixteen and Under, and Mom and Dad are in the Husband-and-Wife dou-bles, even though Mom isn't too good.

"I don't have to be any good," Mom teases Dad. "My partner hits all the balls anyway."

There are divisions for my age, too, and even Betsy could've played in the Girls' Ten and Under, but nobody ever has time to teach us to play. My father and mother both work, and when they're not work-ing, they're driving Stacy and Davy to tournaments.

When we got to La Jolla, I wanted to watch, but Betsy kept on dragging me over to the playground. "Swing me," she said. *"Please,* Dori?"

"I'll swing you fifty times," I told her, "and then you have to let me watch the matches."

Betsy is sweet. She really is; it isn't just a put-on. But she's so cute that everybody does everything she asks them to, so she kind of keeps on being The Baby because it pays off. I'm afraid she'll get spoiled. There's no danger of that ever happening to me.

Betsy and I are a lot different. The family calls us Sugar and Spice. But we kind of look like each other. We both have straight red hair that Mom chops off when it gets down to our wings—that's what she calls our shoulder blades. Betsy is shorter and chubbier than me, and Mom says that if she doesn't quit eating so much candy, she's going to have a weight problem. I like candy, too, but Dad says I'm all bones—that's another thing they notice.

After fifty swings and "just one more slide," Betsy and I went over to the court where Stacy was playing in the finals of the Eighteens. She could have played in the Sixteens, but she's going east to the National Girls' Championships next week, so she needs the toughest competition she can get.

"I sure hope she wins the Nationals," I told Bets, and she said, "Me, too."

My brother Davy was sitting and watching in the stands with all the other people, so we climbed up on the noisy board seats and squeezed in on either side of him. I sure was surprised. Davy never watches girls, especially his sister.

"How's she doing?" I whispered, and Davy said, "Oh, she's way ahead. No sweat."

Davy has curly yellow hair and real blue-blue eyes like Betsy's, not cat-green like mine. I'm the only one

11

of us kids with green eyes and a temper.

But Dad sure has a temper! His hair is *real* red, and he has brown eyes. Nobody can ever figure out how come mine are green.

Stacy was serving. She tossed the ball high, hit it hard into her opponent's service court—that's where the rules say you have to hit it—and ran in to the net. But she didn't have to do anything else, because the other girl didn't even get her serve back.

Stacy is bee-you-tiful! She has dark curly hair and blue eyes like Mom's. Mom wears her hair short, and Stacy's is to her shoulders. She ties it back with a ribbon when she's playing tennis, but wispy little curls leak out around her face.

Davy got bored and left before Stacy was finished, and Betsy wanted to go swing some more, but I made her stay. Stacy was playing great. The other girl couldn't win her serve even once, and Stacy had already won the first set, 6–2. To win a set, in case you haven't been brought up in a tennis family like mine, is to win six games. You have to win at least two games more than your opponent, too, or keep on playing till you do. Sometimes you have to play lots of extra games in order to win the set. Sometimes you play a "sudden death" tie-breaker point to see who wins. I'll explain that later. Anyway, to win the whole match, you have to win two sets.

After Davy left, the black-haired girl from Los Angeles began to catch up. Her name is Rosita Perez, and she's ranked the best Eighteen and Under in southern California. Stacy must have surprised her, winning that first set, but she wasn't surprised anymore.

The score was four games to four, Stacy's serve. Rosita was crouched low, with her racket in both hands, swaying from side to side. She looked so fierce that it gave me the shivers. Stacy let loose with her hardest serve, but Rosita hit it back about a thousand miles an hour.

"Love–fifteen," the umpire said, and Stacy served again. Rosita hit another forehand like a bullet, and it was love–30. If Stacy lost her serve, she would have to win Rosita's. But Rosita was serving great, too.

Stacy just pushed one of those curls up under her ribbon, blew out her breath, and hung in there. Her next serve didn't look hard, but Rosita never touched it. A serve, hit fair, that your opponent can't hit back is called an ace, and Stacy is good at serving aces. The umpire said, "Fifteen–thirty," and then Stacy put in a tricky twist that hopped high on Rosita's backhand—that's her left side, because she's right-handed. Rosita hit it into the net, and it was 30–all.

The next point went back and forth about a million times, till Rosita hit one out-of-bounds. Stacy was ahead, 40–30!

Rosita pulled the score up to 40–40—that's called deuce—with a furious overhead smash when Stacy

13

tried to lob over her head. Then Stacy served another ace. "Advantage, server," the umpire said, meaning Stacy had the *advantage* 'cause she only needed to win the next point to win the game. But the score went back to deuce a couple more times before Stacy won two points in a row for the game.

"Five games to four, Sinclair leads," the umpire announced.

Now Stacy had to break Rosita's serve, and Rosita helped out by starting with a double fault. A fault is when you don't serve the ball into your opponent's service court. You get two tries, and if you miss both of them, you lose the point. It's a dumb thing to do, and Rosita was so mad at herself that she made up for it by serving three aces in a row and getting ahead, 40–15!

Stacy looked kind of worried. If the games went up to 6–all, they'd have to have a tie breaker, and she hates tie breakers. They are sometimes called "sudden death," because you can lose the set, or even the whole match, by just one point.

"Take your time in a spot like this," Dad always tells her and Davy. "Don't rush it." Stacy walked back to the baseline and got ready to receive the serve. Boy, when my sister gets that determined look on her face, you'd better watch out.

Rosita served a twister and ran in to net to volley it away. But Stacy socked the ball in a high arc over Rosita's head for a perfect lob that landed in the backhand corner of the court. Rosita raced back to get it but didn't even come close. Then, at 40–30, still out of breath, she served another double fault, and it was deuce. The next two points were long, fierce rallies, but Stacy won them both—for game, set, and match, 6–2, 6–4.

Gol-lee! Davy should have seen that set.

I wanted to watch Davy's match, too, but the boys' finals were at the Beach and Tennis Club, and Dad had forgotten that he was going to take Betsy and me. So we went to watch Grandma. She'd already been playing about two hours.

"I sure hope she's winning," I told Betsy, and she said, "Me, too."

Grandma has won the Senior Women's every year for almost as long as I can remember. But when we were driving to La Jolla that morning, she said, "I'm afraid I'm about over the hill. This woman I have to play today is just barely old enough to play in the Seniors' this year, and she's mighty good."

My grandmother must be about sixty, although she'd never tell. I figured it out: Dad was twenty-four when Stacy was born, and Stacy is sixteen, so that adds up to forty years. Grandma was probably around twenty when Dad was born, and forty and twenty is sixty. But I still figured Grandma to win.

"Is that the lady from Arizona that's going to beat Grandma?" Betsy whispered to me after we sat down in the bottom row of the stands. You have to keep

15

quiet when you watch tennis tournaments. I found that out when I was littler than Betsy and got yelled at by Dad for making too much noise when he was playing.

"She's not going to beat her!" I whispered back fiercely.

Just then the umpire announced, "The score is six games to six, third set." They would have to play that fluky tie breaker!

Grandma has pretty silver hair, short and curly, and she's thin like me. She can run real fast, but her face was pink, and she looked kind of tired. I was worried about her.

In sudden death, they keep score differently from the regular games. Instead of 0, or love, then 15, 30, 40, and game—*if* you win by at least two points— sudden death goes 0, 1, 2, 3, 4, game, and you can win by only one point!

It went 1 to 0, 1 to 1, 2 to 1, then 3 to 1 for the other lady; 3 to 2, 3 to 3 (Grandma was catching up!); 4 to 3 for the other lady; and then 4 to 4. Just one more point would decide the whole match, and Grandma was serving.

"Come on, Grandma!" I yelled.

I didn't mean to. It just ripped out of my mouth. The umpire turned around in his high seat and glared down at me. All the people in the stands went, *"Ssssshhhh!"*

And Grandma served a double fault! Grandma

16

had lost the match, all because of *me*.

I grabbed Betsy's hand and ran as fast as I could. We ran past the playground and crossed the boulevard. Betsy was crying; she couldn't keep up with me. So I slowed down, but I kept on pulling her after me down the hill to the beach.

When we got to the sand, Betsy plunked herself down with her back against the seawall.

"I can't run anymore," she panted.

"Well, then, stay here," I told her, "and don't move."

I went down to the ocean and ran and ran as far as I could go on the wet sand. I didn't want to ever come back. It was low tide, and the ocean was running out, leaving bunches of wet seaweed. I was crying so much that I couldn't see, and I slipped and fell on a pile of kelp and landed hard on my bottom. It knocked all my breath out of me, but it didn't hurt much. It reminded me about Betsy, though. She gets scared.

When I got back to where she was supposed to be, she wasn't there! So *I* got scared. What if she got lost? I was supposed to take care of her!

I almost panicked, but then I thought, *What could've happened to her? She won't go near the ocean, that's for sure.*

Betsy's been afraid to go into the waves ever since she was two—and that's another thing that's my fault. When I was eight, I dragged her in. I thought

17

she'd like it, but she didn't. Sometimes she has bad dreams about it and screams in the middle of the night, and I have to get into bed with her.

"Please, God, let me find Betsy," I prayed. "And I have to find her before Dad comes, or he'll kill me."

If I found her first, Betsy would never tell on me. I looked up and down the beach—there was no little girl all by herself. I didn't think she'd dare to go back to the tennis courts without me, crossing that busy boulevard. This beach wasn't crowded like the one at La Jolla Shores, but some people were stretched out on blankets on the sand and some were under umbrellas. Maybe she was under somebody's umbrella. She's the world's friendliest little kid, even if she is kind of shy.

"Betsy!" I yelled. "Bet-seeeee!"

But nobody even looked up, and all I could hear was the ocean, roaring in to the shore. I got more and more scared. What if she'd been *kidnapped?*

2 • STAR PITCHER STRIKES OUT

The best thing to do would be to find Dad. I didn't exactly want to; I just knew I had to. Even if he made me do all the dishes for a year, it would be worth it if only we could find Betsy.

It seemed like two miles up that steep hill from the beach. I was all out of breath, and my chest hurt. I had to wait a long time to get across the boulevard, there were so many cars. But when I got in sight of the refreshment stand at the tennis courts, where our family always meets, there was Dad, waiting for me.

"Dad! Dad!" I yelled, sprinting to him. He didn't scoop me up, like he always used to. I'm too old for

19

that, anyway, but I wished I wasn't. He was frowning something terribly. Wait till he found out I lost Betsy. . . .

He already knew! At that moment, she came around the corner of the refreshment stand, eating a hot dog, and when she saw me, she said, "I'm sorry, Dori. I was scared of the ocean. I was scared it would come up and get me."

So she'd come back all by herself, and my dad had seen her crossing the boulevard. Boy, was I going to get it!

"What's the idea of leaving her all by herself?" he roared at me.

"I don't mind," Betsy said. "I'm okay, Daddy." And she took hold of his hand and smiled up at him the way she does.

But Dad wasn't about to let me off, no matter what Betsy said. He gave me a long lecture about Responsibility in front of all those people standing around drinking pop. Then he said, "You're on restriction for ten days."

On restriction! I'd rather do the dishes. When Dad says you're on restriction, you can't do *anything*. You can't watch TV, you can't play with your friends, and you can't go anywhere, no matter what. Dad says that parents who don't teach their kids to be good don't really love them. He always tries to be fair, though, so I said, "What about my team? We have a game on Thursday."

"And Dori's our star pitcher!" Betsy said, bursting into tears.

I wouldn't cry. I wouldn't give him the satisfaction. But I asked if I could have some other punishment so that I wouldn't have to let down my team.

I like softball a lot, and Thursday would probably be our last game. We were tied for second place in the Rock Canyon league, which has twelve teams. If we ended up first, second, or third, everybody on the team would get a trophy. If we lost the game on Thursday, we might not even come in third. If we won it, though, and the first place team lost, we'd be tied for first and get to have a play-off! I was trying to explain all this to my father when Davy came up, all sweaty, and everybody wanted to know how he'd done in his match.

"Did you win?" we asked excitedly.

"Yeah. I was lucky," he said. "Hey, Dad, could you lend me a quarter for a bottle of pop?"

"Drinks on me," Dad said. He was so proud of Davy that he almost popped.

I'm proud of Davy, too, but I had all these mean words inside of me that I couldn't swallow. "Oh, sure," I said, "Davy is the great tennis champion. He never does anything wrong."

"What's the matter with *her?*" Davy asked, and Dad said, "Never mind. Let's get on home."

It was awful riding home in our old blue station wagon with the whole family. I burrowed into a

21

sleeping bag way in the back, because I couldn't face Grandma. But I could hear her when Mom asked her about her match.

"It was close," she said, as if it didn't matter. "I'll beat her the next time."

She didn't tell on me for yelling at her at match point—that's when just one point is needed to win a whole match—and that made me feel even worse. It was my fault Grandma didn't win *this* time, and she wasn't getting any younger.

I don't think I deserved such a bad punishment for not taking better care of Betsy, because she turned up okay, and she'd have been all right if she'd only stayed where I'd left her. Besides, I could cross that street by myself when I was her age. She just likes being The Baby.

This is Betsy's "first year" in Bobby Sox, and she's the bat girl for the team. Ms. García, our manager, calls her our Equipment Director to make her feel important. The other Bobby Sox teams had agreed to let her be a "courtesy runner," too, when we need one, because we have one less player than they have. You're supposed to be from nine to twelve for the minor leagues, but if your birthday is before September, you can play when you're eight, and Betsy is almost only one year younger than that.

Bobby Sox started in 1963 in Buena Park, California. Dad doesn't think it's as important as tennis, but he doesn't know anything about softball! There might not have been *any* girls' softball teams where Dad grew up, in the East. But now there are Bobby Sox *leagues* all over the West, and even in Hawaii, and there are girls' softball *teams,* at least, all over the United States. And if you keep on playing in the major leagues and IGS (International Girls' Softball), you can even turn pro when you're eighteen!

When I phoned Coach Robbins with the bad news that I couldn't play, she said, "Oh, dear. May I speak to your father?" I didn't think it would do her any good. Dad doesn't believe in changing his mind. Anyway, he wasn't there.

"Dori, tell her I'm not coming, either," Betsy whispered.

"What's the matter?" I whispered back. "Are you afraid to go without me?"

"Uh-huh," Betsy answered cheerfully.

"I . . . uh . . . don't know if Betsy can make it either," I told the coach. I didn't think she'd care that much, but she had sixty fits.

"Betsy *has* to come," she screeched wildly. "We need her."

Any baseball team that needs my little sister is heading straight for the cellar. Betsy tries, but she doesn't really care that much. I think all the competitive spirit in our family got used up by the time Mom had Betsy. And Betsy has about as much natural athletic ability as an awkward armadillo—

23

and about as much understanding of the game!

Coach Robbins explained to me that two other girls were on vacation, so if neither Betsy nor I came, we'd have to forfeit the game. She said Dad should call her or Ms. García as soon as he got home.

I hung up the phone and said, "You have to go, Bets. The team needs you."

"They *do?*" she said, and I said, "Yes. You can't let them down."

"Okay," she said, with that big smile.

When Dad came home, I told him about calling Coach Robbins or our manager.

"Well, I've been thinking about that," Dad said. "You have a point, Dori. I can't punish your whole team."

"So I can go?" I asked.

"You may go," he grumbled.

So *then* what happened? *Mom* said I couldn't go! I got a fever that night, and I wasn't going to tell anybody, but Mom always knows because my eyes get pink. My temperature was a hundred and two, so Betsy had to go alone, after all.

I was supposed to stay in bed. Grandma was off somewhere at a tennis tournament. Stacy and Davy had practice matches—they practice their tennis all the time. Dad had to stop by for them at the municipal courts after he got off work, and Mom had to work late.

"But I'll pick you up," Mom promised Betsy.

"And I'll try hard to get there for the last inning."

Ms. García came by to take Betsy to the game. "We sure will miss you, Dori," the manager told me sadly. "We had a good chance to win this one."

Good old Dori, the family chump. First I make Grandma lose her match, then I lose Betsy, and now it'd be my fault if our team lost the ball game. Ms. García is supernice, though. I told her it was only the stomach flu, and she said I should try soda crackers and ginger ale. And she didn't tell Betsy why they needed her so badly all of a sudden.

Betsy never felt so important in her life! But after she drove off wearing her blue and white uniform, waving back at me out of Ms. García's shiny white Cadillac, I found this note she'd left on the dining room table:

> Mom pick Me up at the Bobysoxs fild and pleese dont forget Because i will be allone and I will be scard so pleese! dont forget.
>
> Betsy

Mom only forgot us once, and then she didn't really forget, because it was a mix-up, and she thought Dad was supposed to get us. It *was* scary—they didn't come for us till after dark.

I was kind of lonesome, with nobody home. It sure isn't much fun being Twelve. You're not a child, and you're not a teen-ager. And you have to go to bed almost as early as your little sister, way before you get sleepy. At least, I do. I don't think my parents

25

realize that I'm six years older than Betsy.

Later in the afternoon I felt better, so I got some ginger ale from the fridge. When I looked out the window over the kitchen sink, I noticed that Davy hadn't done his yesterday's yard work yet. He'd better watch out! I don't see why I can't do the yard work. I *hate* housework. I don't see why girls have to do one thing and boys another, but Dad is old-fashioned.

In the living room, I found a big fat book that Mom's been reading, all about pioneers and buffalo hunters. The next thing I knew, the back door was banging. It was Mom and Betsy.

"Dori! Dori!" Betsy yelled. "We won, we won!"

Mom was just as excited. "Betsy did it!" She laughed. "Betsy scored the winning run!" She was hugging Betsy, and they were dancing around the room.

"Gol-lee!" I said. "How'd she do it? What was the score?"

"The score was nothing to nothing in the bottom half of the last inning," Mom announced, like on the radio, "and Susie Kelly was at bat. Betsy was on third, and there was only one out—"

"Mom came!" Betsy interrupted. "She saw me do it!"

"So what did you do?" I asked crossly. I still wasn't feeling so good. *Our team sure did get along without me all right,* I thought. *Mary Belinski must*

26

have pitched a no-hitter. Boy!

"What did I do, Mom?" Betsy shouted.

Mom laughed. "Susie Kelly swung and missed, but Betsy ran home, anyway. The other team's catcher was so surprised that she dropped the ball and couldn't tag her out."

Then they danced around the room some more, and I tried to act as if it was wonderful. So what was wrong with me? It *was* wonderful. Our team had won. We might get to be in a play-off. And if I could manage for a week or so not to wreck somebody's life, I might even get to pitch. That's if they didn't decide to use Mary.

Dad and Davy and Stace came in just then, and everybody kept on raving about Betsy. I felt awful, and the worse I felt, the more ashamed I got. I was a green-eyed monster! I've never felt that jealous before, even if I do have green eyes, but I couldn't help it. I felt so mean that I almost told Dad about Davy not doing his yard work.

After things quieted down some, we had supper. All everybody talked about was Betsy, and Stacy going to the Nationals next week, and some big tournament Davy was going to tomorrow, in Los Angeles.

"You'll have to get up at the crack of dawn," Dad told him. "I can run you up the coast for your first-round match in time to get back to the office, and then Mom and I can come up on the weekend for the semis and finals."

Davy grinned. "So how do I get home if I don't get that far?"

Nobody even bothered to answer. Davy *always* wins. And he gets to stay in ritzy houses with Olympic-sized swimming pools and stables and private tennis courts and wall-to-wall carpet even in the bathrooms.

Then Dad asked the big question: "Did you finish your chores?"

Davy looked like he wanted to duck under the table. "Uh . . . no," he said, almost under his breath.

"What's that?" Dad said, and Davy mumbled, "No . . . I didn't."

"You didn't do your work and you expect me to drive you to Los Angeles?" Dad roared, and Mom said, "George, I think you'd better talk it over. . . ."

So they went to Davy's room. It was Betsy's turn to wash the dishes, and she said, "Dori, could you trade me, 'cause I'm *so* tired?"

"Must be that great run you scored," I muttered, and I refused to trade.

Since Mom works, she has a special time, once a week, for each of us kids to talk to her alone. While Betsy was washing the dishes, and Dad and Davy were in his room, and Stacy was on the phone with her boyfriend, I figured it would be a good time to have my talk. I sure needed it. Mom said it *would* be a good time, so we went into the living room, and I snuggled up beside her on the sofa. Because I'd been

28

so terrible that week, it was hard to begin. Finally, I decided to start with Grandma. I told Mom how I'd made Grandma lose her match and how awful I felt.

"Did you talk to her yet?" Mom asked, and I said, "No, I'm scared to."

Just then Dad came out of Davy's room. "Well, we worked it out," Dad told Mom.

"Does he get to go to the tournament?" I demanded. I *knew* he would.

"Davy is going to do extra chores after he gets back," Dad said.

I jumped up off the sofa and glared at my father. My insides were fizzing like a bottle of shook-up pop. *"That's not fair!"* I yelled, and all the stuff I've been thinking for six years tumbled out of me. "You weren't going to let me play on a crummy old softball team, but *tennis* is *important!* So Davy gets to play even if he didn't do his chores. And Stacy and Davy have been playing tennis ever since they were six years old, and I'm twelve, but you don't ever have time to teach *me* how. All I ever get to do is to take care of Betsy!"

Dad just stood there and looked at me, and it was awfully quiet. His face got redder and redder, and Mom said, "George. . . ."

I figured now I'd really had it. I didn't know what Dad was going to do to me, and Mom looked scared, too. Then you know what he said?

"Game, set, and match . . . to Dori Sinclair!"

29

3 • PROMISES, PROMISES

Dad wasn't being sarcastic, as I thought at first. He really meant, *You win, Dori!* He said he hadn't realized how old I was getting, and that Betsy and I should both learn how to play tennis.

"Me, too?" Betsy asked.

Dad swooped her up and swung her around, answering, "You too, Sugar." Then he said, "Davy, instead of those extra chores next week, you can work out with Dori."

"Me?" Davy groaned and hit his head with the palm of his hand. But he grinned at me, so I guess he didn't mind that much.

The next day, when Mom woke Betsy and me for breakfast, Dad and Davy had already left for Los Angeles. Stacy's boyfriend, Sam, was out on the patio waiting for her to get up. Mom invited him in for some pancakes.

Sam lives around the corner, and he and Stacy have been going together since she was in junior high. He's a couple years older than Stace, and Dad isn't too enthusiastic about having him around so much. Mom likes him okay, and *I* think he's great. He has curly brown hair and brown eyes, and he's practically a giant! He just graduated from high school in June and won a basketball scholarship to USC.

Can you guess what he's going to be? A *dentist!* I guess somebody has to fix your teeth, but I sure hope Sam changes his mind. He's a terrific basketball player, but he says that he doesn't want to be something just because he's tall.

Stacy came to the table in pink rollers, and her eyes weren't all the way open yet, but she still looked beautiful—she *always* looks beautiful. She said, "Hi, Sam," and they talked about Stacy's trip to the Nationals, while Mom kept on flipping pancakes until everybody was full.

Then Mom rushed off to work, and I had to do the dishes. Betsy sat at the table with Sam and Stacy while I cleared the plates off and took them over to the sink. In our house, the table is in the family room, and there's just a room-divider buffet with

31

barstools between there and the kitchen, so I could hear them talking.

Poor Sam! You'd think Stacy was going on a trip around the world instead of just to Philadelphia and maybe New York. Of course, someday she *will* get to go around the world. There are tennis tournaments in about every country you ever heard of.

I could hardly wait for Davy to get back from his tournament to teach me how to play good enough to get into tournaments. I mean *well* enough. (My English teacher would probably kill me if she read this book. But I'm just putting it down the way I talk, okay?)

After I finished the dishes, I decided I might as well go and face Grandma. I had to do it sometime.

"Come on, Bets," I said with a sigh. "Let's go see Grandma."

"Okay," she agreed. *She* didn't have anything to worry about.

Grandma lives in a little cottage that belongs to the big house in the avocado grove next door to us. She'd noticed it was empty and asked the people if she could rent it. She wanted to be close to her family but not *too* close. My grandma believes that if you want something, you should come right out and ask, because you sure as glory won't get it if you don't ask.

It's a neat place to visit, because there's a big old pepper tree in the yard, and Betsy and I use it for a playhouse. I usually love to go over to Grandma's, but not this time. My feet felt like a couple tons of lead.

"Maybe she won't be home," Betsy said helpfully, but I told her I had to get it over with sooner or later.

Grandma was out in back, digging in her flower bed, in the big straw hat she wears to keep the sun off her face. She says she gets enough sun playing tennis and doesn't want any *more* wrinkles. Once, when Betsy was real little, she said, "I love you, Grandma. You have a pretty, wrinkled face!"

Grandma didn't see us right away, but when Betsy said, "Hi, Grandma," she jumped up and came to meet us with both her arms out, the way she always does. So I knew she wasn't mad at me.

"Come on inside, where it's cool," she told us, after giving us both a good big hug. "I'll make some lemonade."

I sat on the edge of her old-fashioned wicker settee and said, "I'm sorry I made you lose your finals, Grandma. I didn't mean to."

"Of course you didn't mean to! You meant to help me," she said. Her blue eyes were twinkling as if she didn't really care, but I knew better.

My dad's mom is where all the competitive spirit in our family comes from. Mom says, "I can't imagine *my* mother chasing around in tennis shoes!" Her mother lives back East, and she only came to visit us once, when I was too little to remember.

"I'm sure glad you live next door to us," I told

33

Grandma, and she said, "Me, too."

The lemonade was great—real sweet, and sour, and tinkly with ice. And I found out something about Grandma that I never knew before. I was explaining why I felt extra bad about making her double-fault on match point. "You *never* double-fault," I said.

"Well, Dori," she said, "it didn't bother *me* any when you sang out, 'Come on, Grandma,' but it might have bothered my opponent. So that was the only thing I could do. Now, don't you bother your pretty red head about it anymore. The next time I meet that lady, I plan to clobber her."

I bet she will, too!

Grandma was delighted to hear about Betsy and me getting to play tennis. "I've been planning to teach you ever since I moved out here," she said, "only I just never got around to it. I can't believe you're twelve years old, Dori."

"Almost thirteen," I reminded her. "Is that too old, Grandma? For me to be a champion, I mean?"

She didn't answer right away. Grandma always tells the truth. "It would have been better if you'd started sooner," she admitted. "But if you work hard enough, and practice all year round, you can still catch up with the kids who started earlier. You're a mighty good softball player, I know, but tennis takes a lot more practice than just about any other sport."

"I'll practice every day," I promised. And says we have to keep our promises.

Promises are easy to make, but not so easy to keep. Davy had promised to work out with me, but when Dad and Mom brought Davy back from the tournament in Los Angeles, they were so excited that they forgot all about me.

Besides winning the Boys' Singles, Davy had entered the men's division, just for practice. But he'd won it! And there was a rich sponsor who wanted to take him to play in the men's division of the Pacific Northwest tournaments in Oregon and Washington and Canada. He'd have to leave in ten days, and he wouldn't be back for a month.

"It'll be great experience," Dad said, and Mom said, "What a wonderful trip!"

"So when is Davy going to work out with me?" I demanded.

Davy looked at Dad, and Dad looked sorry. "That's right," he said. "I don't see how you can go, son. Maybe next year. We promised Dori."

Davy started to say something real loud, then shut up and went to his room. He was in there a long time, and I felt kind of uncomfortable about it, but it *was* my turn.

"I'd teach you myself," Dad muttered, "but I'm working overtime already." He paced up and down the living room, looking unhappy. Then all of a sudden he said, "Dori!"

"Yessir?"

"Get Betsy and hop into the car. Hurry up! We're going shopping."

Betsy was a mess. She had on a dirty old jersey and jeans with the knees out, her face and arms were streaked, and her hair was all tangled. I got a clean dress for her and had just grabbed the hairbrush and a wet washrag, when Dad honked the horn at us. She looked sweet and clean when we got to the shopping center. *I* was the mess.

"If you're going to be a tennis player," Dad said crossly, "you're going to have to pay more attention to your clothes, Dori."

I thought, *If I have to wear fancy dresses and lace panties, I guess I'll stick to softball!*

Dad took us into a huge new sporting goods store and headed for the rackets, a whole wall full of them, hanging up high. Gol-lee! There were hundreds of them: shiny silver steel rackets, soft gray aluminum rackets, and wooden ones, varnished till they were gleaming gold. Dad took down a wooden one and put it in my hand. It didn't have any strings in it yet, which meant they would string it especially for me. Boy, I never thought I'd get a racket like that to *begin* with.

"Shake hands with it," Dad said, and I said, "I know how to hold a racket. At least I know *that* much."

Dad said, "Well, there's still a lot you have to

learn." He was acting kind of cross, as if he was thinking about Davy not getting to go to the Pacific Northwest because of me, and even though I was getting my racket, I didn't feel very happy. I didn't know why.

Dad said, "Heft this one. How does it feel?" I hefted and swung about twenty rackets and said how they felt to me.

"This one's too heavy," I said, and "This one's too big for my hand."

Betsy giggled and said, "You sound just like Goldilocks!"

Dad picked out a special lightweight racket with a shorter handle, already strung, for Betsy—a child's racket. She was perfectly happy with it. Stacy and Davy had started off with full-sized rackets when they were younger than Betsy, and I sure wouldn't have wanted a racket like hers.

Then Dad lifted down a brown-and-gold wood racket with a star on the throat, and the minute I put my fingers around the handle, I knew: *This is my racket.* It wasn't too heavy or too light, and it just fitted into my hand.

I looked up at Dad, and he said, "That's it, huh?" He didn't seem mad anymore. It was as if he knew exactly how I felt. "I remember when I got my first racket," he said.

I didn't want to leave it there even one night, so the girl who strings their rackets did it special for me while Dad picked out some tennis shoes for me and Bets. He said our old sneakers wouldn't do, because when you play tennis, you have to be sure to have plenty of cushion for your arches and to *never* wear shoes that are too short, or you'll get black toenails and sprained ankles and stuff like that. "It'll not only ruin your feet," Dad joked, "it'll ruin your *tennis.*" It sure was nice having my father kidding about *my* tennis, for a change.

When we got home, everybody admired our new rackets, even Davy. He tried to pretend he'd just as soon stay home and work out with his kid sisters as go to the Pacific Northwest and play in the men's tournaments, but Davy isn't all that good an actor. Dad was looking sort of glum again, too.

So I said, "Davy can go if he wants to. I don't care." And I *am* a good actor, so everybody believed me.

Davy shouted, "Yippee!" and Dad said, "He might even win this year," and Mom put her arm around my shoulders and said, "That's very nice of you, Dori."

So how do I get to be a champion? *I'm* not getting any younger, either.

4 • WATCH THE BALL!

I like to lie in bed in the morning with my eyes closed, making up dreams. Like this one morning: I've just finished winning the finals in the Center Court at Wimbledon, and the Queen has invited me to her castle to tea. I'm sitting on a red velvet sofa in the drawing room, talking to the Royal Family, when a funny-faced footman with a white wig like George Washington's and green satin knee britches brings me a crystal goblet full of ice-cold strawberry soda. (That's what I'd ordered.)

The rest of the family is having hot tea, but I don't care for tea, and one of the princesses asks, "Mama, could I please have some pop?"

"Pop!" exclaims the Queen. "Is that what they call it in America?"

"Yes, ma'am," I reply. (That's how you're supposed to talk to the Queen of England after you win at Wimbledon, the most famous tennis tournament in the world.)

Just then there was a loud noise in my ear: "Get up, Dori!" I rolled over and pulled the sheet up over my head.

It was Davy, and he wouldn't let me sleep. He got Betsy up, too, which is even harder. "I've only got five days to teach you how to play tennis," he told us.

I don't know why he had to do it at seven o'clock in the morning, but it was kind of nice, once I was up. It wasn't so nice later, I found out. Whew! I also found out why they call practicing your tennis a *workout*.

We walked over to the high school courts, and they were all empty. It sure was quiet around there. Davy made me hold my racket right. As Dad had said, you're supposed to shake hands with the handle, with the racket face perpendicular to the ground, like a pancake on its edge. The racket should be an extension of your arm, Dad said.

"You don't have to hold it clear down at the end of the handle," Davy told me. "You can choke up on it a little, since you're a girl."

41

"Stacy doesn't choke up on it," I said indignantly.

"Right," Davy agreed. "I only meant for a start."

He had a box full of old balls, and he put me in the middle of one side of the court and stood behind the net on the other side. Betsy sat on the bench, waiting for her turn. About every three balls, she said, *"Now is it my turn?"*

The first ball Davy threw, I hit! It went up over his head and landed right in the court.

"Nah," Davy said. "Not like that. Don't face the net; stand sideways to it, like you're a batter and I'm pitching to you. And hold your racket back."

"Like this?" I asked.

"No. Point it toward the back fence, with your arm out straight. You don't want to have to jerk your racket back at the last minute after I throw the ball. Be ready ahead of time."

I tried it, and the ball went into the net.

"Nah," Davy said. "Don't hit down on the ball. Swing level and hit right through it."

The ball went over the net, nice and low!

"Did I do it right?" I asked. I figured he had to say *that* was okay.

"Well, you should've followed through, with your weight on your front foot, just like in baseball. And let your racket end up pointing to where you want the ball to go." He came around behind me and took my arm and whooshed the racket around a couple of times. "It should end up a little higher than it

42

starts,'' he said. Then he went back and threw some more balls.

I missed the next ball, but the one after that I hit over the net—and I followed through.

"Nah," Davy said. "Don't let the ball get so close to your body. You should hit it with your arm out straight."

"Well, you threw it too close to me!" I retorted.

"What are your feet for?" Davy said. *"Move.* Step away when you see the ball is coming close, and run for it when it's gonna be too far to reach."

The next ball I hit over the fence. "Nah," Davy said. "You're not playing softball." The harder I tried, the more Davy kept telling me what I was doing wrong. "Keep your eye on the ball," Davy growled, like a sergeant in the army.

I don't think I played so bad before he started mixing me up. It's not as if I'd never hit a tennis ball in my life. I'd done it lots of times, whenever I could find an empty court and anybody to play with me. Unfortunately, the only kids who would play were worse than I was, and the people in the next court were not very friendly when we hit too many balls in their direction.

Some people had been polite and said, "Would you kids mind moving somewhere else?" And some had been sarcastic and said stuff like "Come back when you learn how to play!" Where the heck did they think we were going to learn how to play tennis?

43

Finally I sputtered, "Davy, you've told me so many things, and I can't think about all of them at the same time."

Davy said, "Okay, Dori, take a break. You look tired."

"I am not tired!" I ripped out. My big brother was helping me, which is all I ever wanted, and yet I was getting madder every minute.

Anyway, the box was empty, so we had to pick up all the balls. Davy can flip them up with his racket on the side of his shoe, but I can't do that yet, so I had to stoop over every time, and boy, did I get a backache!

"Now can I hit some?" Betsy asked, when they were all in the box.

"I dunno," Davy teased her. *"Can* you?"

She couldn't. I sat on the bench while he threw her a whole boxful, and she missed all but one. But Davy said, "Great swing, Sugar!" and "That's the way!" and "You're gonna be good!"

I looked at the star on the throat of my new racket, and it was all blurry. Why didn't Davy say *I* was going to be good?

Because I wasn't any good, that's why.

All week, Davy hauled us out of bed every morning and threw balls to Betsy and me for three hours. Most of the time it was to me, because Betsy is kind of lazy, and she gets hot. But I didn't get any better. I got worse.

44

"Watch the ball," Davy kept telling me.

"I am watching the ball," I fussed. "Anybody knows that much about tennis."

He called me up to the net and pointed to the little black 2 on the fuzzy yellow ball. "Can you read that number?" he asked, and I said, "Sure I can!"

"Can you read the name on the ball, the name of the company that makes it?" Davy asked next. "Well, read it every time you hit the ball. That's how close you have to watch it. And whether you're hitting for practice or playing a match, never take your eyes off the ball. Don't take your eyes off it to look at the person you're playing, or the spot in the court where you're planning to hit it, or anyone outside the court that's watching or passing by—"

"Not even at a butterfly?" Betsy asked, and Davy said, "Not even if it lands on the ball!"

Every afternoon I practiced hitting against the back of our garage. Dad painted a line as high as the net for me to practice with. He said he'd done that for Stacy and Dave when they were beginners, too.

Ugh! Who wanted to be a *beginner?*

Every night I was so tired that I couldn't go to sleep. Instead of counting sheep, I counted tennis balls, and I *watched* every one. I had some weird dreams—"frustration dreams," Mom calls them. Sometimes my racket didn't have any strings in it, so the balls went right through. Or Betsy and I would keep on picking up balls all day but never fill the box.

45

MATCH POINT

One night, when I was supposed to have cleaned my closet that day but forgot about it, I dreamed that when I opened the closet door, a million fuzzy yellow balls fell out on my head.

Thursday evening, Ms. Garcia called. She was all excited. "They just told me we're to be in a play-off," she said. "The team that was in first place had to forfeit their last game, because some of their players didn't show up, because their car broke down. They tried to reschedule the game, but the officials said it was against the rules. So we're all tied up, thanks to Betsy!"

"Wow!" I said. "When do we play?"

"I'm afraid it's tomorrow, at eleven o'clock. Can you both come?"

"We sure can," I told her, and then I went and told Davy. "Don't get us up tomorrow morning. We need our rest. We're in the Bobby Sox play-off!"

"Fine with me," he said.

I felt kind of guilty, because he was leaving Saturday, so Friday would have been my last chance to get tennis lessons from a real pro—well, practically a pro. But the way I felt by eleven A.M. after a workout with Davy, I couldn't get to first base on a triple—if I could even hit a triple.

I was afraid Dad would say something about my "not taking advantage of this great opportunity" to learn from a top boy player, but he understood how I couldn't let my team down.

46

And I could *play* softball. I thought, *Maybe that's what I'll decide to be a champion of. It looks like tennis isn't my game.*

The next day, Betsy and I slept in. We didn't get up till nine o'clock. Boy, did that feel good! After breakfast, which I cooked, since Mom had to go to work, Ms. García came for us. And what do you know? Davy asked if he could come along!

"You mean you want to watch the Bobby Sox?" I gasped, and he just grinned. Davy doesn't talk much, except when he's telling you everything you're doing wrong. *Gol-lee! I don't know if I can even play softball if* he's *watching!*

5 • THE PLAY-OFF

Our softball team is called the Rock Canyon Radiators, and we wear blue and white uniforms: white shirts and shorts, blue caps with RCR monograms, striped blue and white knee socks, and blue and white shoes. The team we had to play for first place was the Hilltop Hardwares, and they wear black and white. We were playing behind Betsy's school (Rock Canyon Elementary); it has a big flat field of hard dirt, surrounded by a chain link fence. That's all they have for Bobby Soxers—Little Leaguers get grass!

There are two sets of wooden benches—one for the

rooters of each team—separated by a refreshment stand with an "upstairs," where the official score-keeper sits.

"Those parents had *better* be separated," Davy joked when I told him which side he should sit on. Then he said, "By the way, kid, don't take it personally if I leave before the end."

"It's okay with me if you leave right now," I retorted. But I did kind of wish Mom and Dad could have come, or at least Mom. It's tough when both your parents work and only get to come on weekends.

Just as I'd thought, Mary Belinski got to pitch. I was at first. Susie Kelly was our catcher, and Betsy, of course, was on the bench.

The Hilltop Hardwares, being the visitors, were up first. "Hey, hey! Hit it away," their team started chanting.

Mary Belinski hardly ever gets rattled. She's short and thin, with dark braids and black-rimmed eye-glasses, and she takes her time. She doesn't look very good, but she gets them out, one way or another—usually.

Her first three pitches were over the plate but high. The next two were hit foul, for three balls and two strikes.

"Full count," called the ump, with his fists up.

Crrrack! The bat connected, and there was a hard grounder heading for right field—unless I could stop it. It almost knocked me over, but I gloved it and got back to the bag in time for the out.

Mary walked the next batter, and I shouted, "Hey, hey! Double play!"

"Get 'em out if it takes all day!" second base sang back, and the Hilltoppers yelled from their dugout, "Come on, Babe, you can hit it!" And all the parents were screaming at their kids, telling them what to do. Boy, softball sure is different from tennis, where you can't even holler, "Come on, Grandma!"

The third batter tried a bunt, but it wasn't very good. Mary threw it to second, and second base threw it to me in time for the double play.

I forgot all about Davy watching when we were on the field, but when I was sitting in the dugout, waiting for my turn at bat, I got cold chills. Our first two batters struck out. Ramona Rolphe, their pitcher, had been picked for the Bobby Sox All-Stars. She's an American Indian, and she has thick black braids down to her waist. We were hoping that she wouldn't be pitching for the play-off, but there she was.

Susie Kelly was up third, and I was on deck. Susie went up to the full count and then kept hitting foul balls. The suspense was terrible. I looked up at Davy in the stands and chewed my gum fast to keep my teeth from chattering. Davy just grinned and made an O with his finger and thumb.

Crrrack! went that beautiful sound—beautiful

when *your* team's up—and Susie made it to second base on a hard grounder to left field. But now it was up to me to hit her in, and my bat felt like a Ping-Pong paddle.

Facing Ramona, with my whole team yelling, "Come on, Red, you can do it!" and my big brother watching from the stands, I wished I was on the bench with Betsy.

I stood there like a popsicle and let the first two balls go by. One was a strike, and one was a ball. Everybody was yelling, "Hit it!" so I reached for the next one. It was about a foot over my head. Boy, if I kept that up, I *would* be on the bench.

"Watch the ball!" I heard Davy yell.

"Watch the ball!" Coach was yelling the same thing. I guess it works in any sport. Not just look at it, like I used to think, but watch it close. I laid back my bat and kept my eyes glued to the ball in Ramona's glove . . . in her hand . . . spinning toward the plate. . . .

"Meet it," I muttered. "Just meet the ball." But I didn't really think I would.

Crrrack!

Wow! I was so surprised that I just stood there and watched the ball soar into the blue sky. At first, I thought maybe Susie could come in after they caught my fly ball, only there were two outs already, and she was only on second, anyway. But the ball kept on going. Gol-lee! I'd never hit a home run *that* far before.

51

It didn't just go past the chalk line. It went over the fence—and with Ramona pitching!

Susie came home, and I jogged around the bases. My team was jumping up and down and screaming. Coach Robbins is a quiet person, but she hugged me, too, and said, "Nice going, Dori," and Ms. García gave me a *big* hug. It sure makes you feel good to have your whole team hitting you on the back.

After the first inning was over, the score stayed two to nothing till the end of the sixth, and in Bobby Sox, there are only seven innings. Mary wasn't pitching a no-hitter, but we managed to get double plays on the few batters who did get hits, so at least it was a no-runner. And after giving up those two runs to us, Ramona was just fantastic. She retired three batters in a row every inning, striking out at least one of us an inning. I didn't get up again until the bottom of the fourth, and I socked the first ball she pitched, good and hard again, but flied out to center field. I didn't mind so much, though, because I'd never hit the ball that hard before, and it sure felt good. All those tennis workouts with Davy must have helped my softball!

In the top of the seventh, Mary Belinski got in trouble. She'd been doing a great job, but I guess her arm was tired. Or maybe she got nervous because we were only ahead two to nothing. All she had to do was hold them, and we'd win the game. Just hold them that one last inning. I knew how she felt.

Mary walked the first batter on four straight balls, then figured she'd better throw one across the plate. So the second batter connected on the first pitch and drove a single out to center field. It didn't help any when our center fielder bobbled the ball, or she might have caught the runner at third. Mary got wilder every minute. The next three pitches were balls, and the one after that hit the batter. So their third batter went to first, and the bases were loaded with Hilltop Hardwares.

"Hey, hey! Hit it away!" the Hilltoppers were howling as Ramona came up to bat. She's their clean-up hitter, and on the first pitch, she hit a single to right field. Right field threw to the plate to cut off the run, but it was pretty wild, so Susie missed it, and two runs came in. Then when Susie dug the ball out of the backstop and threw to Mary, who was covering the plate, Mary turned and threw the ball way past second, trying to catch Ramona. Only she didn't. Our shortstop and second base collided, trying to catch her throw, and the third run came in. Mary should've just held on to the ball, but she got desperate. I think she was crying and couldn't even see. The play ended with Ramona on third. So they were ahead three to two, and the Hilltop Hardwares bench was yelling like crazy: "Hey, hey! Look at the score! That's okay, but we want more!"

Mary threw three more pitches—three balls—and that's when they decided to let me pitch. I felt like

53

saying, "*Now* you let me pitch."

When I threw my warm-ups, they were as bad as Mary's pitches, or maybe worse. My stomach was churning like a washing machine.

"Come on, Red," Susie called to me from behind the plate. "You can do it."

I looked up at the stands, and Davy was still there. I couldn't believe it. Davy watching a bunch of Bobby Soxers, with all those errors!

"Concentrate," he yelled at me. That's what he always tells himself when he's in a big match and gets disgusted with the way he's playing. He sounded pretty disgusted with me, too.

I stuck my gum in the side of my mouth and took a good look at the batter. I really tried, but my first pitch was high and outside, for ball four. She walked.

"One ball, two balls, three balls, four," their team was chanting from the dugout. "Come on, pitcher, walk some more!"

Our manager won't let us say that one. She says it's not good sportsmanship, and I don't think it is either. It made me so mad that I threw three strikes in a row.

"Yea, Dori!" my team was screaming.

One out, and two to go.

Getting mad doesn't work very long, though, and I got wild again and walked the next batter, so the bases were loaded. Then I got lucky. The next one up

54

hit straight to me. I threw to the plate in time to keep Ramona from scoring, and she was out, but the batter was safe at first. So there were two outs, but the bases were still loaded, and I was still in trouble.

I was facing their ninth batter, and in Bobby Sox the innings are limited to nine batters up, whether you get three outs or not. *So whatever happens,* I told myself, *this is it!*

Sometimes I feel like I'm pitching good—it's my day—but I sure didn't feel that way then. I was still uptight. I got to the full count on their catcher, and then she hit about a hundred foul tips. I kept getting more and more nervous. She's a pretty good hitter, even if she does bat ninth, and if she hit a homer, it would be *seven* to two. . . .

"Concentrate!" Davy was yelling. I guess he could tell I wasn't. I mean, I was concentrating on the wrong thing. Just like in tennis, you have to have confidence and not think you're going to serve a double fault or hit one out of the court, or you probably will.

Keep cool, I told myself. *Don't worry about anybody else. So you're pitching bad? Okay, start all over. Start from the beginning.*

I called Susie out for a conference. "Could you bring up the target a little?" I asked, and she said, "Okay."

"Just watch that glove," I muttered to myself, and I pretended Susie's mitt was a yellow tennis ball.

56

"One ball, two balls, three balls, four," screamed the Hilltop dugout, and I threw my hardest. I threw so hard that I almost fell over.

"Stee-rike three!" called the ump. Three outs!

Whew! *That* was over. Now all we needed was two runs!

Ramona was still pitching, better than ever, and Ms. Garcia had to put little Kim Kimura in, because everybody is supposed to get to play.

Kim stood in the batter's box, looking real serious. Ramona wound up and threw what looked to me like a good pitch, but it just missed the corner. Kim never moved a muscle.

"Ball one," called the ump, sticking his finger up.

Then Ramona threw another one right over the plate. Kim just stood there.

"Stee-rike!"

Being a first-year Bobby Soxer, Kim doesn't have too big a strike zone. In fact, she isn't much bigger than Betsy. Ramona just missed the strike zone on the next two pitches, and Kim kept on waiting. Ramona's next pitch was right over the plate.

"Stee-rike two!" hollered the umpire. "Full count."

Kim held her bat like she planned to hit the next one, but she didn't swing at all.

"Ball four. Take your base," the ump told her, and Kim trotted down to first. Coach Robbins sent Betsy in to run for her so that Betsy could be in the

57

play-off, too. Betsy strolled over to the bag, then turned and waved to Davy.

The next batter struck out, and Susie was up. She socked the first pitch as hard as she could, but it went too high, and their left fielder made a great running catch. So there were two outs, and I was up—with nobody to "clean up" but Betsy. If I hit her in, I'd have to hit a triple, because Betsy doesn't run very fast. And that would only be a tie score, three to three, with Mary Belinski coming up to bat. Like most of the team, she hadn't had a hit all day.

If it was a tie, I'd have to pitch again, and that was the last thing I wanted to do, the way I was pitching. So all I had to do was hit another home run. Ho, ho! Two in one game. I had to be dreaming.

"Come on, Red, Babe," everybody on our team was yelling at me, and their team was chanting, "Hey, hey! Put her away!"

"Keep your eye on that ball!" Davy sang out.

So I watched it as close as I could, the way he made me do about a million times when we were working out in tennis. I was looking for a meaty pitch, straight over the plate and waist high, but Ramona wasn't about to give me anything like that. After she pitched me three balls, I figured she was thinking about that home run I'd hit in the first inning, so she didn't care if she did walk me, with Mary coming up next, and with two outs in the bottom of the last inning. I was thinking about it, too.

58

"Okay," I muttered. "It's now or never."

I stepped back, took a deep breath, then tapped the plate and crouched for the pitch. It was high and outside, but I reached for it.

Plip. This time there was a soft, dull thud. It was probably the first time in softball history that anybody aiming for the fence came up with a bunt. As the ball trickled a little way from the plate and died, I took off for first. If I'd have stopped to think about it, I'd have figured that it was a lost cause—Betsy would never make it to second!

Their catcher threw wild, way past second, and Betsy kept trotting along. I was safe at first, and Bets was safe at second, I was thinking, and by some miracle, Mary Belinski might—

"Oh, no," I groaned.

My little sister was still going. She had rounded second and was chugging steadily toward third. The Hilltop Hardwares were going crazy.

"Get her!" they yelled.

Their shortstop and center fielder had collided over the ball in the middle of the field, so to add to the confusion, I started for second base.

Their shortstop came up with the ball, but threw to second instead of third, so I figured that Betsy would reach there safely. I ran back to first, drew another wild throw, and took off for second again. I got there safe, and by then Ramona had charge of the ball. So there we were—me on second, Betsy on third, with two outs and Mary Belinski at bat.

Mary looked pretty fierce, black braids bristling, eyeglasses glittering, skinny legs spread apart, and her bottom stuck out as she laid her bat way back and swung.

Whish!

"Stee-rike!" yelled the ump.

Whish!

"Stee-rike!"

Crrrack!

Wow! A clean single to right field. Betsy came in. I came in, and everybody was hugging us and screaming, "Yea for Mary!"

The score was four to three, and we were the league champions. Davy came down on the field to congratulate our team, and do you know what? Mom and Dad were both there! They'd taken a long lunch break and watched from the parking lot, not wanting to distract us by arriving late and maybe having to leave before the game was over.

"That homer of yours almost hit the car roof," Dad told me, with a big grin. He swung Betsy up in the air. Then he swung *me* up in the air.

Boy! That sure felt good.

6 • I CAN'T BEAT MY GRANDMOTHER

Around six o'clock, Sam ambled over to our house. I don't think he's been having any fun, with Stacy gone. He looked as mournful as a hound dog.

"Stacy call yet?" he asked, and Dad said, "No. I can't understand it. It's nine o'clock back there. She said she'd call as soon as the finals were over, win or lose."

Dad was pacing up and down the living room. It was a big day. Stacy was in the finals of the National Girls' Sixteens, and he must've been looking forward to it ever since she was six, when he'd started throwing balls over the net to her.

"When does she get home?" Sam wanted to know.

"It depends," Dad said. "She'll be playing in the Girls' Eighteens at Philadelphia in August, and if she wins that, she'll be invited to play at Forest Hills."

"In *September?*" Sam flopped down in our biggest chair, and his legs stuck out halfway across the room.

"Even if she doesn't win today, she'll be second in the United States in the Sixteens, and she'll get invited to a lot of tournaments on the East Coast."

"I know," Sam said sadly. "She told me."

"When do you start college?" Dad asked, and Sam said, "Gotta report September eleventh," as if it was the day of doom.

I knew what they both were thinking. Dad was glad that Sam would be gone when Stacy came home, because Dad is scared Stacy will fall in love and mess up her tennis. Sam is scared her tennis will mess up her falling in love. I don't think Stacy is in love *yet*, but Sam sure is crazy about her.

The phone rang, and Dad plowed up the carpet to get it, but it was only Grandma. She wanted to know if Stacy had called yet.

"No," Dad said crossly. "Get off the line. I'll call you back."

Mom said, "George! That's no way to talk to your mother," and the phone rang again.

"It's Stacy!" Dad roared, and everybody crowded up around him to hear. He held the receiver a little way out, and we could hear Stacy's voice saying, "I won! I won!"

"She won!" Dad was so excited that he dropped the receiver. It hit the rest of the phone and knocked it off the table onto Dad's foot. He yelped, more out of fear that the call was disconnected than out of pain, but when he got the receiver up to his ear again, Stacy was still there.

"What was the score?" Davy asked. "How about the doubles?"

"Is she okay?" Mom wanted to know. That's all she ever worries about.

"Tell her I love her," Betsy said, and I shouted, "Tell her our team won the Bobby Sox play-off!"

"She won the singles *and* the doubles," Dad told us, after he and Stace finished talking. "The score was seven–five, six–four against that girl from Florida, Mimi Castleton. And the doubles was a cliffhanger—seven–six, six–seven, seven–six."

"Three tie breakers in one match," Davy said. "That's *wild.*"

Dad phoned Grandma and told her the news.

"Can I talk to her?" I asked before he hung up.

He handed over the phone, and I said, "Hi, Grandma. Betsy and me won the Bobby Sox play-off, too."

"That's wonderful," Grandma said. "I wish I'd been there. Come on over in the morning and tell me about it."

"Okay," I said. At least somebody was interested.

After Mom told Betsy and me it was time for bed, a pretty surprising thing happened. Davy came into our room. He had his gear all packed for the Pacific Northwest, and he said we wouldn't be seeing him in the morning unless we woke up awfully early.

"You're gonna be pretty good, you know that, kid?" he told me.

I figured he meant the softball, so I said, "Thanks for all that practice, Davy. At least it helped my batting."

"You're gonna be good in tennis, too."

"I am?" I asked, and he said, "Yup. All you have to do is hit a couple billion more balls."

"Forget it," I said. "I'd rather play softball!"

The next morning I woke up early. I must've got into the habit. Mom was in the kitchen. She said Davy had just left, and I got this kind of hollow feeling. I wished he hadn't gone. Davy never paid that much attention to me before, and I even wished we could keep on having those crummy workouts.

I couldn't very well be a Bobby Sox champion when the season was over; and school was out, so there wasn't much else to do. I hauled Betsy out of bed. She wasn't much, but she was all I had.

"Come on, Bets," I said. "Let's go play tennis."

"Okay," she said cheerfully.

We had some breakfast and went over to the high

school courts. Betsy started off great. We even got some balls back and forth across the net. "Nice going," I told her, but in about fifteen minutes, she said, "It's getting hot, Dori, and I'm so tired. . . ."

"Well, let's go see Grandma," I said, with a big sigh. I sure wasn't going to get to be a tennis champion with Betsy for practice.

On the way to Grandma's, I thought about all the times Grandma'd told me that she "was going to play" with me, only she "never got around to it." My grandmother is a busy lady. She's always working in her garden, or going to bridge luncheons, or playing in tournaments. But I had a great idea, and I remembered what she always said: "If you want something, you should ask for it, because you sure as glory won't get it if you *don't* ask for it."

"Grandma," I said, when we found her out in her yard again, "do you think you would have time to play tennis with me if I do your weeding for you?"

"Well, bless your heart," she said, "of course I would."

She said she'd play with me for an hour every morning, before the sun got too hot, and then I could do some yard work for a half hour every day, any time I wanted to.

"That's not fair," I said. "I should work for an hour."

Grandma burst out laughing. "To tell you the truth," she said, "I expect I'm going to like playing

65

tennis with you, Dori. It won't be very long before you'll be good practice for me."

Well! It sure as glory *is* a good idea to ask for what you want.

"See you tomorrow morning at eight o'clock," Grandma said.

When Betsy and I got home, there was Sam spread out on our front steps, looking like a sad-eyed, droopy-eared beagle. And he had a beat-up old tennis racket on his lap.

"You want to hit some?" he asked, and I blurted, "What?" and he said, "Would you like to play tennis with me?"

"Me?" I asked. I just couldn't believe my ears.

"If Stacy's going to be a superstar," Sam told me in that slow way he talks, "I reckon I'd better brush up on my game."

"I'm just a beginner," I warned him.

"Join the club." Sam grinned at me, and I was glad to see him looking happier.

"Okay," I said, "but don't say I didn't warn you."

I felt kind of self-conscious showing up on the high school courts with a six-foot-nine-inch basketball star. (I don't have to look down very far to get a good view of his turquoise and silver belt!) There were quite a few kids around; some I knew, and they looked impressed. Sam'd already graduated, and I'll only be in eighth grade this fall.

A cute blond with gooey eye makeup came up to us and said, "Hi, Sam. I didn't know you played tennis, *too,*" and batted her icky eyelashes at him.

Sam just said, "Hi, Judy. See ya," and kept on walking with me. I mean *he* was walking. I had to run or skip about six steps to his one, and I couldn't help giggling. We sure must've looked funny.

We got the last empty court, and when we started hitting, I noticed Sam wasn't holding his racket right, but I didn't say anything.

"I hear you've been havin' lessons with the champ," Sam said. "Would you mind tellin' me if I do somethin' wrong?"

He bounced the ball and hit it over the net—and I missed it. *Me* tell *him?* "Well, Davy says you're supposed to stand sideways to the net," I mentioned. "If the ball comes on your forehand, your left foot should be in front, and if it's a backhand, your right foot is in front, and when you hit the ball, your weight goes onto your front foot."

Sam tried it and said, "How about that!"

But I decided to quit worrying about all that stuff Davy told me and just concentrate on getting the ball back. After that, we had fun! Sam was kind of wild at first, but he settled down, and I kept my eye on the ball and *ran* for it, no matter where it landed, so pretty soon we were getting the ball back and forth four or five times. Sometimes. And when we quit playing, Sam's face was as red as mine!

67

"Hey, that was all right," he said. "Let's do it again."

"Okay," I said.

"How about tomorrow?" he asked, and I said, "Fine with me."

Wow! I never thought I'd get to play tennis with Sam.

Every day, I played tennis with Grandma, the world's steadiest player, the first thing in the morning, and with Sam in the afternoon. He's the world's wildest! Dad said I had to keep on working out with Betsy, whether she wanted to or not, and I had my regular chores and Grandma's weeding, so the summer was going by real fast.

"How would you like to enter a junior tournament? There's one up near Disneyland next week, and I could take you and Betsy," Grandma said one day.

"A tournament?" I gasped.

Betsy shouted, "Yea, Disneyland!"

"I can't play in a tournament," I said. "I can't even serve yet."

"You've got a week to learn," Grandma said.

"A *week!*" Grandma had been playing sets with me, only I couldn't get my serve in, so she let me hit the ball over underhand. It's pretty easy to get it in that way, but I couldn't do that in a tournament. I'd be ashamed to.

"I'll show you an easy serve to start with," she

68

told me. "Just throw the ball up about a foot over your right eye, bring your racket up behind it, and tap it over in an arc—like so. It's like throwing the ball into the service court."

I'd thought you had to twist your racket around and do a lot of fancy stuff, but the way Grandma showed me was pretty simple. It *is* like throwing a ball, only you do it with your racket.

It only took me one session to learn that serve, but when I showed it to Sam that afternoon, he wasn't too impressed. Sam has a real powerful serve. He winds up a lot, and when the ball goes into your service court, you'd better get out of the way. Only it doesn't go in all that often.

"I'm working on it," he kept saying. "I'll have it by the time Stacy gets home."

Grandma beat me every morning, 6-0, 6-0. Even though she kept hitting the ball right to my forehand (my backhand isn't too good yet), and no matter how many times I hit it back across the net, she never lost a game. Sometimes I got to deuce and even my ad—that's short for *advantage*. One time when it was my ad, I hit the ball just a teeny bit out, and she said I won the game.

"My ball was out," I said fiercely. I don't want to win *that* way. Grandma said that means I'm a real champion.

"You're getting better every day," she'd told me after practice that morning. But if I really was getting better, how come I couldn't win even one game?

"How can I enter a tournament?" I asked her. "I can't beat anybody."

"How about Sam?" she asked me. "Can you beat him?"

"We don't play sets," I told her. "We just practice our shots."

"Well, why don't you try?" she said.

So the day I learned how to serve, I asked Sam if he would like to play a set.

"Okay with me," he agreed.

I figured he'd slaughter me, and sure enough he started off with three aces that whizzed by me so fast that I could hardly see the ball. After that he served two double faults. Then he won the game with another fast serve.

I was pretty sure Sam would murder those dinky little serves I put in, and he did—only he hit them about ninety miles an hour into the net or over the baseline.

"That little old yellow ball looks just like a cream puff," he said, and I said, "I don't care. I won my serve!"

In the next game, Sam served more double faults than aces, so it was 2-1 for me, and then we both won our serves the rest of the set, and it ended up six games to four, *my* favor. Sam looked kind of crestfallen, so I said, "Let's just hit, okay? We get more practice that way."

I never played Sam any more sets after that, and he never asked me to, but we kept on having fun hitting. And the next day I told Grandma that I guessed I would like to enter the tournament. She called up long distance, and we just made the deadline.

Tennis is a funny game. If you practice a lot, you can beat a guy that's a whole lot taller and older than you, and a basketball star besides. And that's even if you can't beat your grandmother!

7 • MY FIRST TOURNAMENT

My first tennis tournament was near Disneyland, about two hours north of Rock Canyon by bus—Grandma didn't want to drive all that way on the freeways. But when we got there, we rented a car. It was a really fun little car, bright red. Grandma let Betsy and me pick it out.

"We're staying at the Disneyland Hotel," she told us. "It's only a short drive from there to the tournament in Santa Ana."

"Can we go to Disneyland now?" Betsy kept asking. *She* wasn't playing in the tournament. She just came along for the rides!

Mom and Dad were always "planning to take us" but "never got around to it." Stacy and Dave went when they were little. They said that I was there, too, but I can't remember. I was in a stroller, and Betsy wasn't even born yet.

Grandma decided that we could go there first and look around. It was Sunday evening, and the tournament started the next day. Grandma was almost as excited as Betsy about Disneyland, but I was worried about the tournament.

"Look!" Grandma said, pointing. "There's the Matterhorn."

I'd seen it before from the freeway, and I wasn't too impressed. It's just a chalky-white mountain sticking up like a papier-mâché ice-cream cone on miles and miles of flat land, and the sky around it, when I'd seen it, was all smoggy-brown. It's a famous landmark in southern California, but it doesn't look like a real snowy mountain from Switzerland. It's fake, but Davy said it has a toboggan ride in it, sort of like a tame roller coaster.

Grandma got our tickets at the gate. You get a book of tickets for all the different rides: the train, pirate ship, steamboat, drive-yourself autos, Mr. Toad's Wild Ride, flying elephants, twirling teacups, stage coaches, and stuff like that.

"And there are lots of good places to eat," Grandma said.

"I'm not hungry," I said, and Betsy said, "Well, I

73

am! I could eat a dozen hamburgers right now!''

"You're not playing in a tournament tomorrow morning,'' I told her. I was pretty cross, but I couldn't help it.

We went into a fried chicken place and sat down at a table. I was thinking that I must've been out of my mind to enter a big southern California junior tournament. It wasn't as if I didn't know how tough they are. I've been watching tennis since I was strapped into a baby seat, and I've never seen any tournament players as bad as I am. I should have started a lot sooner. Or stuck to softball.

''I know how you feel,'' Grandma said. ''It's been a long time, but I can still remember my first tournament.''

''Did you win?'' I asked her.

''No.'' Grandma laughed. ''I got such a pain in my middle that I couldn't play! So you'd best get something into your stomach now. It may be full of butterflies tomorrow.''

Betsy burst into giggles, and I couldn't help smiling a little bit.

''Well, it won't take me long to get my tennis over with, anyway,'' I told them. ''Then I can have some fun.''

Grandma got serious. ''That's no way to talk,'' she said. ''You should never go into a match that you're not determined to win.''

So I got serious too. ''I'll do the best I can, Grandma, and that's a promise," I told her.

The fried chicken tasted pretty good, after all, and then we looked around till the sun went down and the lights came on, all in different colors and streaking through the sky.

"Can we go on the merry-go-round now?" Betsy was pulling Grandma through the castle gates into Fairyland, and you could hear the gay music of the calliope. But Grandma said, "No, honey. The tickets will be good as long as we stay. We'd better go back to the hotel now and put Dori to bed."

Betsy grinned and said, "Okay."

But it didn't do me much good to go to bed early. The mattress was super-comfortable, but I couldn't go to sleep. I kept turning over and punching my pillow. I practiced my relaxing exercises and tried lying on my stomach, but my mind kept on talking. I didn't get to sleep till about two minutes before Grandma called, "Wake up, Dori!"

"Oh, no," I groaned.

She said I had to eat some breakfast, because I shouldn't play tennis on an empty stomach.

"It isn't empty," I told her. "It's got those butterflies in it."

We had french toast, though, and it was *deluscious*—fried crispy, golden brown, rolled in powdered sugar, and topped with dark red boysenberry syrup.

"Going to tournaments would be fun," I decided,

75

"if you just didn't have to play tennis."

I was only half kidding.

In the middle of the morning, the Santa Ana freeway was empty. It's usually bumper to bumper. When we got to the tennis courts, I found out where everybody was! About three hundred boys and girls, all ages, were either already playing on the courts or crowded around the bulletin boards where the draws were posted.

The draws were big cardboard posters with the entrants in each age group matched up in pairs. There were Ten and Under, Twelve and Under, Fourteen and Under, Sixteen and Under, and Eighteen and Under. I was in the Twelves. It's called a "draw," because the names are drawn by lot to make it fair. But first, the officials pick out the best eight players—the ones who won or got to the semis or finals in other tournaments, or who had a high ranking in the district where they played. They're put in certain places in the draw, where they won't play each other right away. These are called the "seeded" players, or "seeds," and they're supposed to meet in the final rounds.

I knew about draws from always looking at Stacy's and Dave's, so I was glad to see that I didn't have to play a seeded player in the first round. If I won, I'd have to play the third seed in the second round, unless she lost in the first round. When seeded

76

players are beaten by unseeded players, it's called an upset. And the person who upsets a ranked player is called a dark horse.

I sure hoped I would be a dark horse!

When my name was called for my match, I was introduced to Jackie Van Arsdale, my first-round opponent. Even though we were in the Twelve and Unders, she looked about six feet tall! Her hair was brown, clipped close to her head, and her short white dress made her long legs look even browner. She said, "Hi," and then clammed up; but her father, who walked to our court with us, was really friendly. That's what I thought then!

He said, "I don't believe I've seen you at the tournaments before, Dori. Are you from the East?"

"No," I said, "this is my first tournament."

Grandma was trailing along, too, and she said, "But you may have heard of her older brother and sister, David and Stacy Sinclair?"

"Oh, yes," the man said. He was even taller than his daughter, and very big around.

When we went out on the court, he was going to go out, too, but Grandma said, "I don't believe parents are allowed to sit on the courts." So they both sat in the stands outside the fence, but I don't think he liked it.

Jackie was scary enough by herself. She never smiled or talked to me, even when we were warming up. After we started playing, she only said, "Fault,"

77

or "Let"—that's what you say when the serve hits the net and dribbles into the service court, and you get an extra serve if you need it—or "Out."

She won the first set so easily that I wondered why she wasn't seeded. She played like a machine, with beautiful strokes, driving the ball first to one corner of my court and then the other. I scrambled back and forth till I was out of breath, but I couldn't win a game; she took the set, 6–0.

In the second set, I remembered something I'd seen Stacy do once when she was in trouble. She explained it to me afterward: "The girl I was playing was a 'picture-book' player. Her strokes were grooved— she wanted to hit every ball at the same height. So if I made the ball bounce just a little higher, especially on her backhand, she couldn't hit as hard, and sometimes she'd even miss."

I figured I might as well try it. When you're behind, Dad always says, "Change your game." It's pretty easy to hit up on the ball a little, when you get into the rhythm of it, and I remembered another thing I've heard from Dad and Davy and Stace and Grandma ever since I can remember: "Keep it deep." Hit the ball way back to the baseline. You don't have to hit extra hard to do that. You just have to figure how to arch it.

Jackie's strokes didn't look half as good when she didn't get the ball where she wanted it. She started missing the corners, and then she got shook and

began to hit weak pop-ups that I could run up to the net and put away. Boy, did that feel good!

Maybe this was my first tournament to play, but I wasn't exactly a stranger to the sport, with all those years of watching. I got ahead, 4–0, and then Jackie caught on. She changed *her* game, and started lobbing instead of trying to hit her hard drives. She didn't quite catch up, though, and I won the second set, 6–4.

In girls' tennis, you get a ten-minute break after you split sets, before you play the third, deciding set. I was feeling great. I never thought I'd even have a third set! Jackie's father gave me one look and marched Jackie off to talk to her. If looks could kill, I'd be dead.

I sat in the stands next to Grandma. I was pretty pooped from chasing after those lobs, and it was a hot day. I took my shoes and socks off and wiggled my toes.

"Nice going," Grandma said. "You used your head." And Betsy said, "Oh, boy, Dori, you played great!"

"I feel sorry for that girl," Grandma told us.

"Sorry?" I cried.

"She's the victim of what is called a Tennis Parent." Grandma took a roll of adhesive tape out of her big straw bag and stuck a piece on the ends of my heels, where my skin was getting pink. It's better to tape *before* you get a blister, and Dad always does it for Stacy and Dave. Grandma also produced a pair of clean socks, which made my feet feel cooler.

"Isn't Dad a Tennis Parent?" I asked.

Grandma smiled. "I reckon he is, at that. But there's a difference between being loyal to your kids and wanting them to win and knocking yourself out to help them, and the way *that* man acts. He's a menace."

I wasn't sure just what she meant by that—until the third set.

Jackie started off serving, and wow! If she kept that up I'd never be able to win her serve. She served two aces, the first one down the middle line and the second way over on the sideline. Her father must've told her to serve to my backhand all the time. I'm working on it, but it's still pretty weak.

Her third serve went down the middle line again, in the same place. I got my racket on it, but I hit it into the net. Then I decided to move way over into the alley and take the next one on my forehand (that's called running around your forehand, and *sometimes* it's okay). But Jackie saw me do it, so she served down the middle, and I never got near it!

Her father told us that Jackie's been playing in big tournaments since she was eight years old. So who did I think I was, trying to beat her? But something inside of me just made me keep on trying. It must be that competitive spirit that Grandma says makes me so mad at myself when I lose.

81

So if I couldn't win Jackie's serve yet, I'd just have to win my own serve till I could figure hers out. I served as hard as I could, and Jackie hit it back even faster. It was right in her groove.

Whoa, I told myself. *Better try one of those high bounces.* So I served a blooper, and she hit it into the net. I kept on arching the ball in until it was 40–15 for me. Then I hit another hard serve that she wasn't expecting. It was an ace, and I sure liked it better than those bloopers. But if I didn't hang in there any old way I could, the match would be over, instead of all tied up at 1–1 in the third set.

We kept on holding our serves until the score was 4–all, and Jackie was serving again. She hit her first serve down the middle line again, but it just barely missed.

"Fault," I said. Her second serve was close, but it missed, too, so I said, "Double fault."

Jackie walked over to serve from the other side and said, "Love–15."

"Wait a minute!" her father roared from the fence. "Just wait a minute. We've got to have an umpire here. *Both* of those serves were good."

I couldn't believe my ears, and Jackie said, "Please, Dad—"

"I'm going up to the desk and get somebody," he said. "Hold your play."

In these big junior tournaments, *nobody* has an umpire until the semifinals and finals. There are too many matches. But you can ask for one if you think somebody is cheating.

Boy! He was calling me a cheater.

Grandma stayed out of it, and Jackie and I sat down on different benches. She didn't say a word, so neither did I. Good thing I didn't tell her what I was thinking about her dad.

In about five minutes, Mr. Van Arsdale came back with another man, who climbed up in the high umpire's chair.

"What's your score?" he asked, kind of bored.

"It's four-all, third set, I'm serving, and it's love-fifteen," Jackie said, like somebody'd wound her up.

Mr. Van Arsdale tried to say something about playing Jackie's first service over again, but the umpire said, "Points stand as played."

Jackie served two more double faults to lose the next two points, for love-40. All of a sudden I knew what Grandma meant. Poor Jackie. She couldn't hit a ball in the court; I think she was crying. She managed to plop the next one in, but I got on top of it and put it away, so it was five games to four, with my serve coming up.

All I had to do was win my serve, and I'd win the match, but I was so mad about being called a cheater that I served a bunch of double faults myself, and it was 5-all. If it went to 6-all, we'd have to play a tie breaker. Jackie began to hit her corner-to-corner shots again, but I ran like sixty and got them back. After a long, hard fight, it was 6–5 for me.

Now get your serve in this time, I told myself, and the first three times, I did. After losing her serve again, Jackie acted like she didn't have any hope. But on match point, I served a double fault that wasn't even close!

"Come on, Dori, you big dope," I muttered. "Don't throw it away."

My next serve wasn't much, but it was in, and Jackie acted like she couldn't even see it. She swooshed her racket as hard as she could, but she missed the ball.

"Game, set, and match to Dori Sinclair," announced the umpire.

I won!

Jackie came to the net to shake hands with me, and she *was* crying. At first I figured it was because she'd lost, but then she said, "I'm sorry, Dori. I wish my dad wouldn't act like that." So I knew it was because she felt ashamed.

"You're a wonderful player," I told her. "I just got lucky."

"No, I'm not, really," Jackie said. "I hardly ever win, and Dad gets so disappointed, and—and I *hate* tennis!"

I didn't know what to say, but I wished I could think of something. Her dad was waiting at the gate, and they walked away together. He didn't say anything to me. Good thing. I sure didn't want to talk to *him*.

That afternoon we went to Disneyland to celebrate. We went on just about everything, and it sure was fun. My favorite was the Jungle River Boat, where you go past tigers and elephants on the banks, and gorgeous orchids in the trees; and under a waterfall; and crocodiles come up in the water and your guide shoots them, *crack–crack,* just when you're not expecting it. Betsy almost jumped out of the boat. But, of course, those animals are fake, and the guns only shoot blanks.

Betsy liked the merry-go-round best. She would have ridden around on those horses all day, going up and down and around and around, smiling and waving at Grandma. Grandma said we could take the rides. She couldn't. "My stomach is getting too old," she told us.

The last thing I went on was the teacups. "I'd rather go on the flying elephants," Betsy said. I tried to coax her to go with me, but she wouldn't. I got in one of the cups by myself and spun around, and there was a sort of steering wheel in the middle of each cup, so I could make it go faster and faster.

I was feeling kind of green when I staggered out of my teacup, but I wasn't about to admit it. "That was fun," I said, "but I guess we'd better go back to the hotel, because I have to upset a champion tomorrow morning."

MATCH POINT

I don't want to talk about what happened the next day. I played Kerry Kendall, who was only eleven. She was the dark horse who upset the third-seeded player. She also beat me 6–0, 6–0.

Afterward, Betsy wanted to go to Disneyland again, but all I wanted was to go home. Grandma said we might as well stay till the bus came, so Betsy went on some more rides.

I sat on a bench in the town square of Disneyland, U.S.A., and listened to the streetcar horses go clop-clopping around. It was a very sad sound.

"I'm quitting tennis," I told Grandma.

"I know," Grandma said. "I quit, too, when I was your age. Several times."

She was teasing me, but it wasn't funny!

"I'm quitting for good," I said.

"Well, in that case, why don't you and Betsy use up these last two tickets?" Grandma said. "Then we'll head for home."

So we got on a raft and went over to Tom Sawyer's Island. It has a tree house and secret caves; on any other day, it would have been fun to explore.

"Did you have a good time?" Mom asked when we got home, and Betsy said, *"Superfabulosis!"*

"It was okay, I guess," I told everybody. "It was nice of Grandma to take us."

You have to be a good sport.

PART TWO

8 • THE FATHER AND SON

It was fifteen shopping days before Christmas, and Dad and Davy were on the grandstand court at the La Jolla Beach and Tennis Club, playing in the National Hardcourt Tennis Championship, Father and Son Doubles. They were in the finals, and if they won, they'd be Number One in the United States.

Mom and Grandma and Betsy and I were in the grandstand watching. Boy, was I proud of my father! Davy's used to being in finals, but Dad has never made it past the semis in a big tournament like this.

"He's been dreaming of this since he was six," I

heard Grandma whisper excitedly to Mom.

Mom looked worried. "I hope they win."

"They'll win," Grandma said.

Dad is always teasing her. "Optimist," he'd say, and she'd say, "Just you wait and see."

She sure is an optimist—she still thinks that I'm going to be a tennis champion! I haven't played in any tournaments since Disneyland, a year ago last spring. I really did quit, but Grandma likes me to work out with her, and it's kind of fun. She beat that lady I'd made her lose to, so now my grandmother is Southern California Senior Women's Champion. I bet she could be the best in the world, but she says she's had enough traveling for one lifetime. I sure haven't. I haven't been anywhere, except Disneyland, and that's too close to home to count.

I haven't beaten Grandma yet, either, but I'm working on it. We've been playing just about every day for a year, and yesterday I had her 5–4, 40–15 in the third, but she hung in there and won, 6–4, 4–6, 7–5. At least I didn't *throw* it away.

And I'm going to beat her tomorrow!

I'm also teaching Betsy, and she can get the ball back and forth a lot of times if I hit right to her. Betsy isn't too old for a beginner, and I'm trying hard to get her to enter the Ten and Unders this year. If I could've started as young as Betsy, then I'd have a chance. I'm doing okay in softball, but you can play tennis all year round. And if you get to be a top pro, you can make over a million dollars—just for playing a *game!*

Dad and Davy had had to win four rounds in the Father and Son to get to the finals, and they'd almost lost in the first round. They'd been down 1–4 in the second set after losing the first, but they'd caught up! Wow! Davy'd played out of his mind. Dad said he hadn't been much help that day; after that, he'd got better. They'd beaten teams from San Francisco, Los Angeles, San Diego, and Arizona.

In the finals, they were playing Frederick Farnsworth, Jr., and Fred III, who came all the way from Massachusetts. They've been Father and Son Champions for three years. Mr. Farnsworth's a big man with white hair. He's kind of a take-charge guy. I don't like him much. He seems a lot older than Dad, and Fred III is in college.

"Fred's number two on the Harvard tennis team," Davy told us before the match, and Grandma bristled and said, "Well, *you've* been winning tournaments since you were ten."

"Oh, I'm not worried," Davy said, grinning at her.

Davy never worries, but *my* heart was drumming like bongos when it was Dad's turn to serve. The score was one game to two in the first set, and he got behind, 15–40! Everybody else had won their serve, and in doubles, that's extra important. And it's super-important to win your very first serve. If Dad couldn't, he and Davy wouldn't have a chance.

Davy went to the baseline to talk to Dad, then ran up to net again and stuck his fingers out behind his back in a signal. Dad got his first serve in, not too hard, and then crossed over to Davy's side of the court. Mr. Farnsworth returned the serve to where Dad was supposed to be, but Davy dashed over and banged the ball right at Fred III's feet. That's called poaching, and it's risky, because your opponent might hit the ball to where you just left.

Dad was so tickled with Davy that he served his best American twist and won the point for a score of deuce. They lost the next point after a long hard rally—Dad was up at net with Davy, and Fred III trapped him with a heavy topspin lob. So it was ad out (the Farnsworths' advantage). But Dad got the next point for deuce again, and after a whole lot of deuces and ads—my dad is very stubborn—he won the game! So Dad and Davy did have a chance.

Everybody held serve till 5-6, and Dad was serving again. If he lost his serve, the set would be over. Mr. Farnsworth returned Dad's first serve with a high lob over his head. Dad and Davy ran back to the baseline together, but couldn't overtake it, so it was love-15. Then Fred III returned the next serve with a cross-court chip that caught Dad at his feet as he was coming to net to join Davy. Love-30. But I still figured they'd catch up.

Dad tossed the ball up for his serve. Then he

caught it and tossed it up again. Then he bounced it a bunch of times.

"What's the matter with Dad?" I asked Grandma. He acted like his arm was made out of tin.

"I'm afraid he's got The Elbow," Grandma said. That's when you're scared you're going to lose, so you do lose.

The Farnsworths climbed all over his weak serves. Davy poached and made a couple of great saves, but it was hopeless. Dad couldn't hit a thing.

"First set to Mr. Farnsworth and Fred," announced the umpire. Mr. Farnsworth acted like he knew they'd win it all the time.

"I hope Daddy's elbow gets better," Betsy said.

Fred III started the second set off with a mean kick-serve that bounced high on Dad's backhand. Dad had had trouble with those all through the first set, but he kept on trying. This time he was ready for it and surprised Mr. Farnsworth by hitting it right at him. Mr. Farnsworth flubbed it into the net.

Everybody clapped. There weren't many people in the grandstand from Massachusetts!

It looked like Dad was disgusted with himself for psyching out on the first set. I never saw him hit the ball so hard, and he couldn't seem to miss. But Davy wasn't playing so well now. He was trying too hard to win—for Dad, I think, because the Father and Son isn't all that important to Davy. He kept making errors, serving double faults, hitting his volleys into the

93

net, trying to poach when he shouldn't. . . .

They got behind 1-3 in the second set. Dad won his serve, but Davy didn't! When they were toweling off at the net post, changing courts, Dad had a talk with him to settle him down. But by that time, Fred III was serving again, and *nobody* could break *his* serve. The score would be 4-1, I was thinking, when Dad got his racket on a blistering flat serve down the center line and just managed to dump it over the net. Fred III charged in, dug the ball out of the cement, and got it back. But he had to hit the ball up, which is suicide in doubles.

Davy got on top of the ball and punched it cross-court into the alley. It barely nicked the outside of the line, but Fred III said, "Good shot." He seemed like a nice boy for having such a Big Shot father. It was a good thing, because Dad and Davy both played out of their minds and took his serve! So it was 2-3 instead of 1-4. Then Davy won his serve, for 3-all.

The next three games were fast and furious, with all four players at the net most of the time, exchanging volleys. (A volley is when the ball is hit back over the net before it bounces. A half-volley is tricky, too. That's when you hit the ball back right after it bounces, while it's still close to the ground.) The ball hardly ever touched the ground. Boy, I sure would like to be able to do that. I like playing net. If I ever get to be a good tennis player, that's what I'm going to do. I'm not going to stay in the backcourt and just whop-whop-whop all day long!

Dad and Davy won the second set. It was 6–4. Stacy and Sam sat with us for the third set. I don't know where they were before. They're always going around holding hands and kissing and stuff like that when Sam comes home from college on weekends.

Everybody kept winning his own serve in the third set, till it went to a tie breaker, at 6–all. The umpire said it would be a twelve-point tie breaker. That means that after the first point, each player serves for two points on his turn, and you have to score at least seven points and be two points ahead before you can win, instead of just one point like in sudden death. They call this *lingering* death!

That's a good name for it. Fred III served an ace to Dad for the first point, and then he won a half-volley shot from his shoestrings when Dave served, so it was 2–0 for the Farnsworths. Davy served an ace himself on the next serve, and Dad, at the net, won Mr. Farnsworth's first serve, so it was 2–all. Then it went to 3–all, 4–all, 5–all, 6–all, 7–all. My cheeks were burning, and my hands were icy. Each time someone was ahead, it was match point!

Eight-all, 9–all. Then, at 10–9 for the Farnsworths, Fred III drove the ball straight at Davy's pocket. But Davy twisted his racket and somehow got it back and won the point, for 10–all! At 11–10 for Dad and Davy, Mr. Farnsworth hit a short, high lob that Dad should have smashed to the baseline for

95

the match, but Dad got The Elbow again and hit it into the net. Eleven–all.

The sun was going down, and it was getting chilly. My teeth were chattering so hard that I almost bit my tongue. Dad served—and he delivered an ace! That was the only ace Dad served, and it really shook Mr. Farnsworth up, because it was his serve next, and *he double-faulted!*

Dad and Davy won, 13–11! "Game, set, and match," announced the umpire, "to George Sinclair and David."

9 • CHRISTMAS GLOOM

After the Father and Son, at the awards ceremony, Dad and Dave got a CB radio, with an engraved silver plaque on it. Davy let Dad have it. Davy already has a bunch of portable radios, electric clocks, silver pitchers, and stuff like that.

"Thanks," Dad said. "This is my number-one lifetime favorite trophy." He sure was happy.

Dad has a few trophies, but Stacy and Dave have so many that they quit counting them, and they're all over our house, even in the bathroom cupboards. After you get out of the Juniors, you can make a lot of money, except that the U.S. Tennis Association doesn't allow cash prizes until you're eighteen, unless you turn pro.

We were expecting to stop at a hamburger stand on the way home, but Mr. Farnsworth invited us—our whole family!—to dinner at the Marine Room. It's a superelegant restaurant on the seashore, with huge windows that the ocean comes up to when there's a storm; but it was low tide then, and the beach was dark. Still, you could see the long line of frothy white breakers turning over and over all the way up the coastline, and the lights of a ship out on the horizon. It was beautiful.

Fred III was pretty good-looking, with dark eyes and a nice smile, but he didn't say much. His dad did all the talking.

Mr. Farnsworth has a big, booming voice, and he didn't skip one of us.

"So," he said to Mom, "you work, eh? And still manage to raise five children?"

"Four," Mom told him. "Sam is my daughter's friend."

"Oh, ho, I can see that!" He wiggled his bushy white eyebrows at Stacy and Sam. "Going together, eh?"

Then he turned to me. "Another tennis champion?" he asked.

"No, sir," I said.

"She's an All-Star pitcher in the intermediate league," Mom informed him, the way she always brags about us whenever she gets a chance.

Then he picked on Betsy. "And this is the baby?" he asked.

Everybody expected Betsy to give him one of her big smiles and just giggle, but she said, "No, sir. I'm eight years old."

Boy, was that a surprise!

The dinner was superdelicious, and if Mr. Farnsworth had quit there, everything would've been okay. But he started in on Dave.

At first it was kind of exciting. He was talking to Dad about a Father and Son tournament in New Orleans right after Christmas, and he said that Dad and Davy should go. He could make arrangements for their housing, and they could even bring the family.

Gol-lee! New Orleans!

But Davy said, "Thanks anyway, but I can't. I've got basketball practice."

"Basketball!" Dad hollered, even louder than Mr. Farnsworth.

Basketball is a bad word to my father. He thinks Davy will get water on the knee or something and wreck his tennis if he plays any other sport. He doesn't want Dave to go out for *anything;* but my brother can get stubborn, too. When he was a little kid, he made a deal with Dad that he wouldn't play Pop Warner football or Little League baseball if Dad would put up a hoop on our garage door and let him shoot baskets. He shot so many that he got to be a superfantastic basket-shooter.

That was fine with Dad . . . till Davy made the high school varsity team. Since then, it's been Trouble.

Dad was telling Dave, "I told you there would be conflicts," when the waitress came to ask us what we wanted for dessert.

I ordered a chocolate sundae and almost fell off my chair when Betsy said, "No, thank you." The waitress didn't hear her at first, so Betsy said it real loud: *"Nothing."*

Wow! Betsy is supposed to watch her weight, but she always makes exceptions. This was a huge temptation, and nobody could believe it.

"He called me a butterball," Betsy whispered to me later. "I don't like him."

She meant Mr. Farnsworth, and she did end up losing all that baby fat, so I guess he did some good in our family. But he sure did wreck our Christmas.

On Christmas Eve, our living room looked just as cheerful as ever, with a crackling fire in the fireplace and the tree in front of the picture window; the lights reflected against the black sky outside, so that it looked like two Christmas trees. But *we* weren't very cheerful.

After a bunch of big arguments, Dad and Davy were barely speaking to each other. Dave said that he had a right to decide what he was going to do with his life and that he might even play basketball in college.

That almost killed my dad. Some big universities, like Princeton and Stanford and UCLA, have been writing to Davy about tennis scholarships, and we all figured that the only problem was which one he'd choose. But he has plenty of time, because he's only a junior in high school. Grandma told me, when we were playing tennis one morning, that Davy was a lot like Dad had been when he was seventeen.

"Boys get independent at that age," Grandma said. "They don't want their parents telling them what to do all the time. They have to grow up."

She told me that Dad had a tennis scholarship, all expenses paid, when he went to college, only he had to give it up. His father died, and he had to get a job and support Grandma and the rest of the family, because he was the oldest.

If Dad had stayed mad, I wouldn't have felt so bad, but he quit yelling at us. No matter what we did, he acted like he didn't care. He just went around the house looking sad.

We always sang carols on Christmas Eve, so we did it now, too, but nobody had any spirit. " 'Tis the season to be jolly" was not true at our house.

Last year I was as excited as Betsy about presents; but this year, there wasn't anything that I wanted. They were bound to give me clothes, because I'm too old for toys, and I already have a bike.

"Who wants *clothes* for Christmas!" I said, when everybody was asking what everybody wanted.

"*I* do," Davy said.

"What clothes?" I asked.

"Oh, shirts and pants," he answered. Shirts and pants for Christmas. That's all he could think of!

Then Stacy said, "Well, you can all spend your money on me. I need *everything.*" She meant for her hope chest.

So on Christmas morning, when Betsy cried, "Wake up, Dori, wake up," I said, "What time is it?" and she said, "I don't know, but it's Christmas!" I just burrowed under the covers. I knew it was going to be a terrible Christmas.

And it was. It was the only bad Christmas we ever had. I did get clothes, and they weren't too bad. Grandma gave me a neat tennis dress that she'd made herself—not too fancy. She never gives up on me going to the tournaments, and I was thinking that maybe I *could* surprise Dad and be a champion—to make up for Davy playing basketball. Then I opened my present from Dad.

It was a bunch of golf clubs.

Dad said, "We'll go out sometime this week, Dori, and I'll teach you to play golf."

But his voice sounded like he was still thinking about how he and Davy could be playing Father and Son in New Orleans, and I thought, *He doesn't think I have a chance to be a tennis champ.*

"Who wants to play golf?" I ripped out. "You're always saying that's a dumb game."

Then I got scared. I figured he'd put me on restriction for a month. All he said was, "They can be exchanged."

Gol-lee! That wasn't like my dad. I wished he *had* put me on restriction.

And Stacy had to pick that minute to show us the ring Sam gave her.

"Are you engaged?" Betsy squealed.

"I sure am." Stacy showed her teeny little diamond to everybody. She was so happy that she didn't notice how Dad was feeling. She never notices anybody but Sam anymore.

Dad got up and walked out of the room. Mom went after him, and pretty soon they came back. Mom told us afterward that she'd told him that Stacy wouldn't be able to get married for a long time, because she had to finish high school that year and then go to junior college. She's going to be a dental technician. Ugh! That's worse than a dentist.

Then Stacy said, "We might get married this June."

"This June!" Dad roared. *"What about Wimbledon?"*

Boy, was he mad! He was just like his old self. You have to be one of the best players in the world to get invited to Wimbledon, and Stacy was getting to go this year. I didn't blame Dad for blowing up. If I could play tennis like Stace, I sure wouldn't get *married*.

103

10 • THE "BOYS' " TENNIS TEAM

The day after Christmas vacation, an announcement came over the intercom at Rock Canyon High: "Everyone interested in trying out for the tennis team is to meet in the boys' gym at three o'clock."

So after school, that's where I went. I'd never been in the boys' gym before, and it's really neat. They have lots more equipment than we do, and the PTA mothers are making a stink about it. But I don't care much about the ropes and parallel bars and stuff like that. I like to play games.

I tried to get a couple other girls to go with me. I've seen them out on the courts, and they aren't too bad. They giggled a lot outside the gym doors, but they wouldn't go in. You'd have thought it was a cage at the zoo!

The gym was empty except for a bunch of boys standing under the basketball hoop at the other end. It looked like a couple of miles across that varnished yellow floor, and I wished I didn't have to walk down there all by myself.

"Chicken!" I told myself. "What can they do?"

I would have had on my tennis shoes, but I didn't know about the tryouts till I heard the public address. My hard leather soles made echoes all the way, and by the time I got to the boys, they were all looking at me.

"You've got the wrong address, Red," one of them said, and they all giggled like a bunch of girls. I almost blew my top, but I figured that was what they wanted me to do, so I didn't.

"I came to try out for the tennis team," I informed them. "Is this the right place?"

"It's the right place," the tallest one told me politely, "only it's the boys' tennis team." He had crinkly gold hair, and he seemed kind of nice. But he was the *only* one.

"There isn't any girls' team," I pointed out, as if they didn't know it. "And I already have permission from the coach."

Coach Hannigan had seemed kind of doubtful, too, but I didn't mention that.

"Coach got called away," the nice boy explained. "He told us he couldn't make it today."

I might have left and come back another day, but somebody said, "She's a freshman, I bet," and a big-around black guy chortled, "Fresh*woman.*" And they all burst out giggling again.

Boys sure can be silly.

"I just want to try out," I said. "If I can't beat anybody, naturally I don't get to play."

The nice boy turned out to be the captain from last year. They called him Jimmy. "Wait a minute," he told me. "We'd better talk it over." And he got them off into a huddle to have a conference.

I couldn't hear everything they said, but I caught snatches, like *"I'm* not gonna play her" and "You gotta be kidding."

When they broke up, most of them headed for the tennis courts, swinging their rackets. They didn't say anything to me, but Jimmy came over and said, "I'm afraid the consensus is that you have to start at the top. I'll be glad to play you a set, if you don't mind my being number one."

"Fine with me," I said, "only just one set wouldn't be fair. How about two out of three?"

Jimmy grinned and said, "Okay. How about after school tomorrow?"

The next day, I got to the courts on the dot of three and watched Jimmy coming across the field.

106

He has a real springy walk, and his gold hair kind of floats up and down with each step. Davy told me that they're in the same physics class, so he figured that Jimmy is a junior. He wasn't sure, though, because there's a special program for gifted kids, and Jimmy's in it.

"He's a whiz at math," Davy said. "In fact, he's pretty good at everything."

"How about tennis?" I asked, and Davy said, "Well, he's not a tournament player."

Davy can't play on the school team because he's always practicing for tournaments during the school tennis season in spring. That's one reason he wanted to go out for varsity basketball—so he could get a letter.

I was glad to hear that Jimmy wasn't a tournament player. Maybe I *could* beat him! But if I couldn't, I'd just have to play well enough to persuade him to let me try somebody else.

For the "boys' " tennis team, I sure wasn't going to wear the dress Grandma'd made me for Christmas. I'd rather wear a shirt and shorts, anyway. And I parted my hair in the middle and tied it in a hank over each ear. But I still must've looked okay, because when Jimmy came up to me, he said, "Hey! It might be nice to have a girl on the team, at that." Then he turned sort of pink and said, "Okay, let's go."

At first, there wasn't anybody else around, and I

107

was hoping the guys wouldn't show up. After we'd rallied for about three minutes, Jimmy said, "You ready?"

I was so nervous that my arm was as stiff as a board, and I'd have liked to hit a while longer. But I wasn't about to admit it. "Sure, anytime," I said.

We spun our rackets for serve or side, and he won it. "You want to serve first?" he offered.

"No, thanks. I'll take the other side." I didn't want to start serving with the sun in my eyes, and you're supposed to change courts after every odd game—after the first, third, and fifth games, and so forth. The sun gets pretty bad on our high school courts at this time of year.

Jimmy didn't even take any practice serves. He just tossed the ball up, and wham! The ball came in deep, right in the middle of the service court, so it wasn't on my forehand *or* backhand. I hate to admit what happened: I couldn't get out of the way, and I fell over backward.

Jimmy was worried. He came up to the net and said, "Hey, I'm sorry. I forgot. Are you okay?"

"Of course I'm okay," I said crossly. What did he mean he forgot? That I'm a *girl?*

I picked myself up and went over to receive in the backhand court, and this time I stood way back by the baseline, so that I'd be ready. So what did Jimmy do? Just plopped his serve in easy!

It was way too short for me to reach, so it was

108

30–love for Jimmy. He kept on serving like that—just like I serve to *Betsy!* I was so mad that I really plastered his next serve for 30–15.

"You don't have to worry about serving hard," I told him. "I just didn't have my footwork going yet, so I lost my balance. It didn't hurt any." (Just my pride.)

But he didn't hit any more hard serves in that first set. He won the first game, and then I won my serve, because he seemed to have trouble returning it. He said he'd never played a girl before, and I noticed that the easier I served, the farther out he hit it. So we were both serving about half speed, but I wasn't doing it because I was afraid of knocking him over! Dad says *strategy* is the name of the game.

We both held serve until 4–all, and that was when the other guys started to arrive. It would have been okay if they'd gone onto the other courts and played their own matches, but no, they had to watch us.

They would've stood along the edge of the court, but Jimmy made them sit down on the benches. He couldn't make them shut up, though. High school kids don't know anything about not breaking your concentration.

"Wow! Look at that serve!" they jeered when Jimmy sent over one of his soft ones. "Be careful not to blow her off the court."

Thank goodness they hadn't been there when I fell over! I guess they must have bothered Jimmy even

more than they did me, though, because he lost his
serve. So I had him 5-4, and I decided to show these
guys a thing or two. Instead of serving the way I had
been winning my serves, I wound up and blasted my
first service deep down the center line, in the corner.
Jimmy was so surprised that he didn't even go for it.

"Yea, freshwoman!" the boys yelled.

But the next time I served hard, Jimmy was ready
for it, and he walloped it back with a heavy topspin
that bounced so crazy that I missed it completely. My
racket just whizzed through the air, and the guys
laughed their heads off.

I didn't catch on till it was 15-40 for Jimmy that I
wasn't being smart. "Never change a winning
game," Stacy'd told me, and that's what I was doing. I could lose my chance to win the set. So I let up
on my serve again, taking my time and making sure
to get it in on Jimmy's backhand—*his* weakest shot,
too.

He got it back, but not very well, and I saw my
chance to run in to net and volley it away. So it was
30-40. I did the same thing again, and the score was
deuce. But Jimmy is not your average dumb guy.
He'd be expecting my next service to land in the same
place, so I tried a twist serve that Grandma had been
teaching me. He wasn't expecting it, so he missed it
altogether, and it was my ad.

Set point! I thought. But it's better not to think
about the score. I got so tight that I threw the ball up

110

four times before I could make a decent toss, and then I hit two serves into the net. Deuce again.

"Oh, no," I muttered. "Not The Elbow *now.*"

The boys were whooping it up on the sidelines, but it kind of helped me. It made me more determined. I put in another twist serve that Jimmy hit into the net, and then, on my ad again, I went back to the deep, slow serve to his backhand.

He returned it, though, crosscourt, real hard to the baseline. It was so deep that all I could do was pop it up in the air, and there it sat, all ready for Jimmy to smash it away. He has a great smash.

"Kill it!" somebody yelled at him.

No wonder he missed it. I bet he could have killed *them.* Anyway, I'd won the first set. I thought, *I should have taken his offer and just played one set. Then I'd be on the team.*

Jimmy looked pretty grim. He told the guys that if he was to be captain of this team, he would suggest their getting in some practice. So, after a little grumbling, they spread out on the courts and started playing their challenge matches to see what number they would be on the team. One good thing about my starting at the top: If I could beat their number one man, I wouldn't have to challenge anybody else.

If I could. Jimmy wasn't about to concede. In the second set, he forgot all about those Betsy serves and really did blow me off the court. For a guy who still has what Grandma calls a "beginner's backhand,"

112

he sure has a strong forehand and a super overhead and serve. He's good at the net, too, except he misses some because he swings at the ball instead of just reaching out and punching it over. He seems like a natural athlete who's never had any lessons.

The way he won that second set, he didn't need any. He came to net behind his serve every time and volleyed the ball first to one side and then—if I managed to get it back—angled it off to the other side.

He also came to net after returning *my* serve. Since he hadn't done that the first set, I didn't have any answers. I tried passing shots and only made one. He's so tall that when he spread his arms out, he just about covered the whole net. Well, anyway, it seemed like it.

Of course, I tried to lob. I don't *like* to lob, but when your opponent crowds the net like Jimmy was doing, you'd better hit it over his head. I didn't lob very well, though. The first couple I tried were short. I couldn't have set up a better smash if I'd tried. So I hit higher, and Jimmy jumped up in the air for them. He looked kind of awkward, with his legs and arms spread all over, but he got the ball and angled it out of my reach.

By the time the set score was 5–2 for Jimmy, I was hitting my lob straight up to the sky. I pretended I was playing Sam, and Jimmy isn't that tall. But Jimmy wouldn't give up on a single point. If he couldn't reach the ball, he raced back to the baseline, got behind my high bounce, and barreled it back. It was kind of discouraging, and I lost the set 6-3.

Jimmy said, "You getting tired? Want to finish it tomorrow?" and I said, "No, thanks. Not unless you do."

So we got a drink at the fountain, and sat down a minute for Jimmy to towel off. He sure was sweaty! I didn't exactly mind sitting down, myself.

"You're good," he told me.

I almost asked, "For a girl?" But I didn't. He was nice, not like the others. I wanted to have him for a friend.

I was still thinking about how I could win the third set, though. Grandma said that was how I finally got so I could beat her—by using my head. Plus my hard ground strokes and coming to net. Because no matter how hard I hit my forehand, she always gets it back, unless I hit it where she isn't.

Jimmy started off in the third set just as good as ever: serving hard, returning all my serves no matter what I tried, and covering that net like a high wall with barbed wire on top. He forged ahead 3-0; I had to do something. With all the practice I'd had in the second set, I began to haul off and sock my lob just like a ground stroke, only higher. You can't baby a lob or it'll go short, or, even if it's deep, your opponent has time to run around it. He can't do that if you put more zing on the ball.

114

Another thing was that at 3–0, I knew I *had* to lob, whether I liked it or not, or the match would be over. I was committed to it, and it began to pay off. Some of my lobs went over kind of low, just where Jimmy couldn't handle them. If he tried to race them back to the baseline, the ball got there first, and he got all out of breath so that he'd miss on the next point, too. Pretty soon it was 3–all.

The other guys were finishing their matches, and they were straggling back, two at a time, to see how we were doing.

"Look at the little lady lob!" one guy hooted, and another gibed, "Sock it to him, sissy!"

Jimmy wasn't paying any attention to them this time, and I tried not to. No matter what they thought, if I had to make "sissy" lobs to win the match, that's what I was going to do. Besides, all the top pros, including the men, say an offensive lob is one of the best weapons you can have. I felt like stopping to tell them that, but if I lost my concentration, I'd be dead. When you're going out for the boys' tennis team, winning is what counts.

And I won, 7–5 in the third, when it was almost too dark to see. I really fought, and when Jimmy came up to the net to shake hands with me, he said, "Welcome to the team."

He was only being polite. The other guys crowded around him, kidding him about losing to a girl.

"Get lost, will you?" he said and walked off by

115

himself. His steps were dragging, and I felt sorry I had to beat him. I almost wished he'd won.

Nobody else spoke to me except the big-around black guy.

"Congratulations," he told me. "How'd you like to take me on next?"

He's as tall as Jimmy, and he looks like he weighs about twice as much as I do. He's not fat, just big all over. He didn't sound too friendly.

"Fine with me," I said. "How about tomorrow?"

But I didn't feel as good as I'd thought I would. I'd made the team, but nobody wanted me on it. Not even Jimmy.

11 • SOME PEOPLE CHEAT!

Just when I started going to tennis tournaments, Dad quit on us kids.

He and Davy were having another big fight about basketball. It was Stacy's eighteenth birthday, on Valentine's Day, and we were all sitting around the table eating ice cream and cake—Dad, Mom, Stacy, Davy, Betsy, and me. Grandma and Sam were there, too.

Mom kept trying to change the subject, but it wasn't all that easy. Stacy is always glad to talk about her and Sam's plans, but that's like waving a red flag in front of Dad!

MATCH POINT

So I tried. "The boys on my team are getting along better with me now," I said. "I won my challenge match with Jeff Saunders, but he didn't seem to mind a lot. On match point, he broke his strings on a smash, and when we shook hands, he said, 'Hey, that was kind of a *bad break!*' and laughed like crazy. He's the one who called me a fresh*woman*. He sure is corny, but I like him."

Davy could have helped out by telling them that Jeff is the editor of the school paper and is about twice as big as I am, but he wasn't even listening. Neither was Dad.

I couldn't blame Davy for getting mad. Dad had just told him that he was only an *average* high school basketball player, but he could be the best in the world in tennis.

"Yeah," Davy answered, "and if I don't make it, you'll be disappointed. I've had it with tennis!"

"Very well," Dad said. *"Do* your own thing. All of you kids, go ahead and do what you want to. It's about time I started living my own life, like your mother is always telling me to."

He pushed his piece of birthday cake away, backed his chair away from where he always sits at the head of our table, and walked out of the room. Davy got up and went out the back door, banging it behind him.

Everybody else was quiet.

We finished our cake, only it didn't taste good

118

anymore, and Stacy went off with Sam.

Grandma said, "It's hard for parents to realize that their children have to grow up."

"Especially fathers," Mom said. Then she pushed back her chair and went to cheer up Dad.

I don't think she did, that day. But the next week, my parents joined a tennis club and started spending all their weekends playing what Mom calls "fun mixed doubles" and Dad calls *"club* tennis," meaning it's pretty bad. But he seems to be having a good time, anyway. They have "ladders," where any club member can challenge the others to find out who's the best, and Dad went right to the top in the "A" men's singles.

"I'm halfway up the ladder in 'C' women's," Mom said, "and still climbing."

Mom is having a ball.

Dad said, "Well, at least I got to be a U.S. Father and Son Champion before I retired to the boondogs."

"That's boon*docks,"* Grandma told him, but Dad and I like boon*dogs* better. Now that he has his "new philosophy on life," as he calls it, we're getting along better. And he doesn't fight with Davy anymore.

Grandma finally talked me into going to tournaments again, and she signed me up for the Long Beach Juniors in March. But Grandma had an important Senior Women's Championship tournament at the same time, Davy *wouldn't* go, and Stacy

119

doesn't play in the Juniors anymore, so I had a problem: I didn't want Dad to know about it. I wanted to surprise him, and I figured he and Mom would be busy at their club, anyway—so how was I going to get there?

Maybe I *couldn't* go. But you can't be a really good tennis player without tournament experience. Grandma finally had me convinced of that, and Jimmy said so, too. He's trying to get the guys on the team to enter some local tournaments that have beginner and intermediate divisions.

"You can learn more about tennis in one tournament than in a dozen practice matches," Grandma said, "even if you lose. Most of the top players in the world lost their first tournament matches. You have to know how to play under pressure, against all different kinds of players on all kinds of court surfaces, and know how not to make excuses if it's windy or hot or starting to rain. And no matter how you feel that day, or how badly you think you're playing, *you have to want to win.*"

"Well, I'll be playing against other schools," I told her. "I sure want to win for my team."

"Same thing," Grandma said. "Team matches will help you win tournaments, and tournaments will help you win team matches."

Win is Grandma's favorite word.

So I said okay, and she lined up a bunch of southern California tournaments for juniors: Long

Beach and Santa Monica in March and April, Ojai (that's oh-HI) in May, and the Southern Cal Junior Championships—the big one—after school lets out in June.

"By that time," Grandma said, "you'll be winning." She said I'm the best junior girl she's ever seen who *isn't* playing in tournaments.

I wish Dad would share her confidence. He said that maybe if I'd gone on playing tournaments when I was twelve, it might not have been too late. But now I'm fourteen, and lots of kids my age started playing in tournaments in California when they were six or eight.

"But tennis is a great game for all ages," Dad told me, "whether you're a champion or just play for fun." Boy, has he changed!

"Well, I'm going to be a champion *and* have fun," I informed him.

And I decided that I was going to Long Beach, even if I had to walk. I planned to win it, too. Who wants to wait till June?

I figured out how to get there: I went on the bus. Grandma arranged for me to get housing, and the people I stayed with met me at the bus station and drove me to my rounds. The Osbornes are really nice—a whole family of tennis players, like ours—and they have a daughter in my age division.

Shelby is super. She has dark curly hair, cut short, and real sparkly eyes. We were friends in five minutes flat. When we went to look at the draw, I was glad she was on the other side, because I didn't want to have to try to beat her. But it turned out that she didn't care all that much about winning tournaments; she just liked to play in them. "If they didn't have any losers, there wouldn't *be* any tournaments," she said, laughing.

She knows Stacy and Dave—she knows everybody! "You've got a good draw," she told me. "I've never heard of the girls in your first two rounds, so they can't be very good, and then in the quarters, you'll probably play Jackie Van Arsdale, if she makes it that far."

"Oh, no!" I cried, and she said, "You don't have to worry about Jackie. She's pretty good, but her father always manages to foul things up."

"I know," I said. "I played her before. He's awful." I wasn't exactly looking forward to meeting *him* again, but maybe Jackie wouldn't get to the third round, the quarters. I sure do feel sorry for her. It's better to have your dad think you're no good than have him following you around all the time, making scenes.

In the semis, I'd probably have to play the second seed, Luellen Jarvis, but Shelby said she isn't all that good. "She butters up the officials and gets to the semis by hook or by crook, but in the finals, Janice always beats her easy."

Janice Kristal is the top seed. "She's a lefty,"

Shelby told me, "and she's real good."

We went over and sat in the stands to watch some early matches till it was time for us to play. The Boys' Eighteens were starting, and I wished Davy was there.

"Your brother is super," Shelby said. "Maybe I could stay at your house sometime when there's a tournament down in San Diego."

She was just kidding, but I said, "Sure. Be our guest," and invited her down for the La Jolla in July. I wished she *lived* in Rock Canyon.

We both were called to our matches at eleven o'clock.

"Good luck," Shelby said.

"Good luck!" I echoed.

We had it, too. We both won our first round, 0 and 0 (that's 6–love, 6–love). Being on your high school team gives you more confidence, I found out. I didn't even get nervous.

We both lucked out in our second round, too, but it was closer. Then the Osbornes took us out to dinner, and we went to bed early, so we'd be in good shape for the next battle. Every round gets tougher. But that night we decided to be doubles partners in the next tournament, and we had so much to talk about that we didn't get to sleep practically all night. We were sound asleep, though, when Shelby's mom came to get us up in the morning.

I was dreading the match with Jackie, even though

123

I thought I could win. We checked the draw, and she had won her two first rounds, but when I went up to the tournament desk to check in, they told me I had won by default! That's when the person who is supposed to play you doesn't come or is injured and can't play or is thrown out for misconduct or something.

I wondered what had happened. Nobody knew, but I bet it was her father! He must have done something *awful*.

I watched Shelby's match and rooted so hard (under my breath) that I was more tired than she was, but she lost. "You know, that's the best I've ever played," she said, as happy as a winner. Then she started telling me about Luellen Jarvis, my next opponent. She didn't sound like a very nice girl, but Shelby said I could beat her if I didn't let her psych me out.

The semis and finals were on the second weekend, so I got to go back. The Osbornes wanted me to stay with them again, and I figured I'd have to go up on that smelly bus that takes three hours.

My parents were in a club tournament, but Mom said that it wasn't all that important and that they could drive me. She was real excited about my winning three rounds, but I still didn't want to tell Dad. I wanted to wait till I won the whole tournament.

He didn't suspect anything. Mom said he figured when I wasn't around that I was staying overnight with a girl friend. Well, I was!

Mom agreed to stay at home and play in the club tournament, so he wouldn't ask too many questions the second weekend either. "Then you can surprise him," Mom said. "He'll be so happy!"

"I thought he didn't care about tournaments anymore," I said, and she said, "Oh, yes, Dori, *he cares*—he just isn't about to admit it."

I didn't have to go on the bus again, though. When Stace and Davy found out about it, Stacy said she and Sam would drive me up on Saturday, and my brother said he'd come and get me after the finals on Sunday. Davy didn't even say *if* I won on Saturday.

"When do I get to go to a tournament?" Betsy asked, and I promised her I'd teach her how to serve in time to go to the next one. Her ground strokes are pretty good now. She's as steady as a clock.

"They have Ten and Unders in the Santa Monica Younger Boys' and Girls'," I told her, and she was really excited. Betsy's going to be nine this summer, and she's had lots more training than I had, so maybe Dad is going to get a *couple* of surprises.

When you're in a tournament and you're winning, you feel great! Everything is wonderful—like your brother and sister being so nice to you, and your best friend rooting for you—and it's the most beautiful day you've ever seen, a sunny spring day without any wind.

That's the way I felt when I went out on the court

125

to play Luellen Jarvis. I was surprised that we were playing on a back court, since it was the semifinals, but I guessed that nobody'd ever heard of me, so they'd figured it wouldn't be a good enough match for the grandstand court. Ha! I was going to be a dark horse! I just knew I would.

Shelby's whole family, and Stacy and Sam, were there to watch me, although they had to peek through the door because of those green windbreaks on all the fences. I guess they think nobody wants to watch you on back courts.

We had an umpire, a white-haired man with black sunglasses, but no linesitters. The umpire said that we could call our own lines and that if there was any question, he would make a ruling. "Is that satisfactory to both of you?" he asked us.

Luellen smiled at him and said, "Sure, Mr. Carruthers. With the best umpire in the business, who needs linesitters?"

I didn't even know his name before she said it, and Shelby had told me to be sure to have linesitters when I played Luellen. "She's about the *only* one you need 'em for," she'd said. But what could I do? I didn't want to make a fuss.

So I just said, "Yes, sir."

Luellen had long yellow hair, held back with a wide band, and she was wearing a pale blue, crocheted tennis sheath. I had my hair tied over each ear with those elastic things, circled with green beads. I

126

wore Grandma's Christmas tennis dress, which was white with green panels in the skirt; it looked kind of homemade, but I liked it a whole bunch better than Luellen's dress.

I wasn't feeling so great anymore, though. I was so nervous that I almost threw up!

After we got started playing, I was okay. It was fun playing Luellen . . . at first. She hits the ball good and hard from the baseline, but she doesn't like to go to net, so we had these long, fierce rallies, cross-courts, and down-the-lines, trying to pull each other off the court, so we could make a placement on the other side.

But if one of her balls fell short, I went to net and put it away! At first, I went in too soon, and she hit past me. She got ahead, 2–love, winning both her serve and mine, and then I remembered what Grandma always told me: "Be patient. Wait for a short one. *Then* go in."

After that, I won six games in a row!

"Game and first set to Dori Sinclair," announced the umpire, "six games to two."

I could see what Shelby meant about having line-sitters, though. At least four times, Luellen called my shot out when it was way in. That only made me more determined to beat her. I knew if I blew my cool, she could win; but that was the only way, so I held my temper.

In the second set, she changed her tactics. She

127

began to dink. Dinking is just getting the ball back soft, without putting any power into it; and since you never hit for a winner, you never miss—you wait until your opponent gets impatient or misjudges his timing and hits it out.

It was smart of her to change a losing game, but I didn't lose my head and play her game. I kept on hitting hard and rushing to net when I could. I made about sixty per cent good shots and forty per cent errors, but the way Luellen called them, it was the other way around! So pretty soon she had me 4-love, and the umpire sounded like he was glad.

It wasn't easy to hold my temper when she made a bad call every time she needed the point for a game. Her long gold earrings glinted in the sunshine, and she kept smiling—and dinking—and calling my good shots out! I hated earrings, I hated dinking, I hated the umpire, and boy, did I hate *her!*

So I blew my top, and she won the second set, 6-0!

When I went off the court for my ten-minute break, Stacy was furious. "I tried to get you some linesitters," she told me, "but they said you have to ask for them yourself."

"So ask!" Shelby told me. She was practically crying, and her parents were indignant, too. They said they would go with me to the desk.

"But why did the umpire let her call my shots out every time they landed near the line?" I asked. "Does he want her to win?"

"Oh, no. Mr. Carruthers is as honest as they come," Shelby's father said. "But he can't see as well as he used to, and he doesn't want to admit it."

"If Luellen hadn't gotten him to call the match, she'd have thought of something else," Shelby sputtered. "They ought to have a tournament for cheaters!"

The tournament desk sent us some linesitters, and Luellen stuck her lip out a mile. Then she turned around and smiled at them. I supposed they were her friends.

But I was wrong. They called every ball correctly, and if we'd had them sooner, I could have won the match in straight sets.

The only trouble in the third set was me. I didn't care anymore about winning the tournament, or surprising Dad, or being the best Fourteen and Under in southern Cal. I just wanted to beat *her*. And I was so anxious to beat her in a hurry that I lost my timing, and I rushed all my shots. My legs felt like lead pipes, but I still overran some of the easiest balls and hit them out of the court. The linesitters didn't have any trouble deciding—they were *way* out.

The worse I played, the worse I felt; and the worse I felt, the worse I played. You can't play tennis if you're depressed—you get all droopy, and you can't move. You can't serve if you think you can't, and your drives won't go in if you're afraid you'll miss the lines. I knew that, but I couldn't help it. I

130

couldn't stop thinking, *I* can't *lose to* her!

Finally, I told myself, *Come on, Dori, you dope. Just keep your eye on the ball and your mind on the game. And* fight!

I fought so hard that I didn't know what I was do-ing, and I pulled up from 1–5 to 4–5. I was playing well again, but Luellen was serving for the match. I saved nine match points—Shelby told me that afterward—and on the tenth, after I got back her hardest serve, she lofted the ball right plunk on the center of my baseline. It bounced so high that all I could do was make a desperate stab and hit it high in-to the air. Luellen ran to net, and, anticipating she'd hit her overhead to my backhand corner, I ran the wrong way. She smashed to the other side, but I raced over and made a forehand crosscourt place-ment on the run.

Wow! My best shot of the day. At least I *thought* it landed on the sideline, but the linesitter called "Out!"

I must've been wrong.

"Game, set, and match to Miss Jarvis," the um-pire announced, "two–six, six–love, six–four."

12 • WE'RE A TEAM!

Coach Hannigan is a short, peppy old guy with grizzled hair and leathery brown skin. He and Dad wouldn't get along very well, because Coach goes all out for jogging to strengthen your legs, running to improve your wind, doing push-ups to exercise your shoulder and arm muscles, and squeezing balls to develop your wrists. Dad says the best way to get in condition *and* improve your game is to play tennis— about five hours a day.

Of course, when you're going to school, you don't have five hours a day, so Coach has a point, and we all agreed to do what he said. We had to, or we wouldn't be on the team very long.

The week before our first high school match, we were all jogging around the track. Tryouts were over, and there were nine guys on the varsity—that includes Maria and me. After I made the team, several other girls tried out. Maria was the only one who made the varsity, but a couple other girls made jayvee. The boys are still pretty uncomfortable, but they're getting used to us.

The number one spot was still undecided between Jimmy and me. He'd challenged me back and won after a three-hour battle, but I didn't concede. He has to play me again! For now, though, I'm number two; Jeff is number three; Harry, Larry, and Carlos are four, five, and six; Maria's number seven; and Fred and Gregory are fighting it out for number eight. That's important, because in the county leagues, each high school fields a team of eight: two doubles teams and four singles players. So number nine is on the bench, and the jayvees can challenge him, too.

It was a cold, windy day, and I could think of a lot better places to spend it than sprinting around the track. I was keeping pace with Maria and Carlos for a while, till I decided three's a crowd and dropped back. Jimmy went steaming around the first lap and caught up with me on the second. His second, my first. With those long legs, he can run awfully fast.

"How's it going?" Jimmy asked.

"If I'd wanted to run," I grumbled, "I'd have gone out for the track team."

"Don't worry. Coach'll get this out of his system in a couple weeks. Besides, we have to practice for our match with Hilltop."

Jimmy settled down to a slow trot, so I had a chance to find out some things I'd been wondering about. "How does it work? Who do I play?" I asked him, and "Do we play singles *and* doubles?"

"Our two doubles teams play their two doubles teams two sets each," he told me, "and we get four points for every set we win. Each of our singles players plays one set with each of their singles players and gets one point per win. That way, the doubles matches can bring in a total of sixteen points, and the singles also add up to sixteen, or thirty-two points altogether. Get it?"

"I guess so," I said doubtfully. "Can I play singles?"

"Well . . . I don't know," Jimmy said. "The way we did it last year, and the way we got the most points, was to put our strength in our doubles teams. If we can get sixteen points there, we only need one set in singles to get seventeen points and win the match."

"You mean I would play doubles with you?" I hated to ask, because what if he didn't want to play with a girl for a partner?

"No." But he grinned at me. "That would be *too*

134

much strength. We have to spread ourselves out. If we each play with a weaker partner, we'll have strength on both teams. Think you can carry . . . uh . . . Maria?''

"I bet you can't get any of the guys to play with her," I said scornfully.

He turned sort of pink and then laughed. "You got me!" he said.

"I'll play with her if that's the best way," I told him.

"We'll see what Coach says." Jimmy didn't notice it, but he was running faster again. It was tough to keep up with him, but I wouldn't admit it. My heart was pumping so loud that I thought he'd hear it, and my sides ached. But I figured it was good for me. Coach ought to be satisfied—I sure was getting in condition.

I broke my record in push-ups, too, and when I got home that night, I was stiff and sore all over from our team workout.

"If this is 'condition,' " I told Mom, "I wish I'd never gotten into it."

Mom gave me a hug and suggested a good hot bath, but I could still feel my muscles aching all night long.

The next day, Coach Hannigan announced our team strategy, which is supposed to defeat all the other teams in our league, even if they have better players.

135

"Harry, Larry, Carlos, and Maria will play singles," he told us. "Jimmy and Jeff will play number one doubles, and Dori and the winner of the challenge match between Fred and Gregory will play number two doubles."

Gol-lee! The weakest members of the team. I'd rather play with Maria.

Everybody looked surprised. Coach Hannigan is the kind of man you don't disagree with, unless you want your head bitten off, but I didn't see how I was going to win those important doubles points with Fred *or* Gregory. Fred is as wild as an unbusted bronco, and Gregory has about as much confidence as a wet noodle.

"When those guys play each other," Jeff said, "it's a question of which one *loses* the most points."

I went up to Coach after we broke up and said, "I've never played much doubles, sir. Maybe I'd do better in the singles."

"You made the team, young lady," he told me. "Now you want to be the coach?"

"So let Fred and Gregory both play," I muttered. "I quit!"

Luckily I didn't really say it out loud, so I'm still on the team.

It was a good thing I didn't blow it, because Coach sent Jimmy over to help me out. He sat down on the bench where I was cooling off.

"We think Gregory would be your best bet," he

136

told me. "He'd be the one most likely to keep out of your way."

"Yeah, I guess so," I admitted. Fred would be all over the court, hitting everything out.

"Okay, let's go work on Gregory," Jimmy said.

We jogged over to the far court, where Gregory was practicing his serve. He's always practicing his serve, and it's not bad. But when he gets into a match, he freezes and can't hit anything.

"Hey, Greg, you're looking great!" Jimmy said, and I said, "That's a good serve for doubles."

"It is?" Gregory joined us at the net post and asked, "How come?"

"Well, you take a fast serve like Fred's," Jimmy told him. "Assuming it goes in, it doesn't give the server time to get in to net to join his partner."

"The important thing in doubles is to get your first serve *in,* my dad says," I told him, and Jimmy said, "Yeah, and her dad is Number One in the U.S. Father and Son doubles."

We really did a number on him, and the next day he beat Fred for the number eight spot.

"All it takes is a little confidence," Jimmy said.

Boy, was Gregory happy!

Gregory is kind of a pale kid, with thin, whitish, short-cut hair and light blue eyes. He doesn't look as if he's been out in the sun very much, and he isn't as big as I am. He's a freshman, too. We're the only ones on the team.

"I never thought I'd get picked to play on the varsity," he told me, when we played our first practice match.

"You didn't get picked," I reminded him. "You won your challenge matches."

He has a nice smile, and he acts like a little brother. I was glad he wasn't going to take all my shots, the way Fred would've, but I sure hoped he'd take *some*. The doubles court isn't exactly narrow.

Coach sent Larry and Harry over to play against us. Yeah, you guessed it, they're twins. They have brown hair, as curly as a couple of dust mops, and you can't tell which one is which. That can get confusing, so we call them both by their last name, Higgins.

"Hey, Higgins," I called, after we'd warmed up for a long time, "how about starting?"

"*I* dunno how to play doubles," they both said.

"To tell you the truth, I've never played much doubles myself," I admitted. "But I can keep score."

It wasn't like the Father and Son! But we played three sets, and it was kind of fun.

Larry and Harry won the first set, 6–2, mostly because each knew what the other was going to do. Greg and I didn't have any idea.

"That's okay," I told him. "We're just not used to each other yet. That's why we're having a practice match. We'll get better at playing together."

138

"I'm sorry," Greg said. I wished he wouldn't keep apologizing. I wasn't exactly playing inspired tennis myself.

The trouble was that I had defeated Larry and Harry in singles so easily that I figured we ought to be able to beat them in doubles, so I was pressing. Jimmy warned me not to do that, but I didn't know what he was talking about till it happened. It didn't help any to have Coach Hannigan hovering over us, either.

After the first set, he called us over for a conference and gave us some tips on strategy.

"You're beating yourself," he told me (not Gregory). "Don't forget, every time you make an error, they get the point. Just play steady and let *them* make the errors."

My face got hot, but when I thought about it, I realized that Greg hadn't missed very many. Of course, he hadn't hit very many either, but I had tried to win all by myself!

In the second set, I asked Gregory if he wanted to serve first. But Coach yelled, "No. Strong serve first, always. That can make the difference between six-four and four-six."

I knew that. I was just trying to be nice, but there was no way I was going to please Coach Hannigan. "He never wanted a girl on the team in the first place," I muttered.

I served my best, and we got off to a good start,

139

1-0. Then, on the first point of the second game, Higgins (whichever) presented Greg, who was receiving in the deuce court, with a double fault.

Afraid of making another, Higgins looped his next serve into my ad court—the court on my right—and there it sat, looking like a big fat balloon for me to burst. But after Greg got that first point by just standing there, we had the game in the bag, providing I didn't foul it up by not getting my point every time. So I just returned my hardest forehand deep to Higgins's backhand. But he didn't have a backhand yet, and there wasn't time for him to run around it, so it was love-30. Greg missed on the next service return for 15-30, but I made my point again, and it was 15-40. Even if Greg missed again, it would be 30-40, and I could win the next point for game. But Greg made a careful return that Higgins hit into the net, and it was 2-0 for us.

Greg looked over and gave me a shaky smile.

"Way to go," I said and smiled back.

We won the second and third sets, 6-3, 6-2, by letting them make the errors, and Coach said, "Good work." I have to admit that it was his strategy that had worked.

On the day of the Hilltop match, I woke up to the gentle drip of spring rain.

"Oh, no!" I cried. "Not today!"

By afternoon there was some blue sky showing between the big white clouds, and the Rock Canyon

High School varsity squad was off for Hilltop High.

Hilltop is even farther out in the boondogs than we are, and their courts aren't very impressive. Besides being crisscrossed with lines for every other sport you can think of, they have a six-inch-wide bump running between the service line and the baseline of the court they picked out for our doubles—and there were numerous puddles left over from the rain. We mopped up all we could, but we were bound to have a bunch of damp purple balls before long.

Purple balls! I don't know where Hilltop came up with those. Coach Hannigan was pretty disgusted. They use yellow ones now in the sanctioned tournaments, because they're easier to see, but *no* self-respecting tournament would use *purple.*

The guys Greg and I played first, their number one doubles team, looked big and clumsy, but they were better than I thought they'd be. They polished us off in the first set without much trouble, 6–2. Greg couldn't seem to get started, and he was so miserable about "letting down his team" that he only got worse. Like Grandma always says, "You can't play tennis with a droopy racket."

Jimmy and Jeff were playing Hilltop's number two team in the next court—the team we'd have to play after our two sets were over. Our team was doing okay over there.

"No sweat," Jeff reported as he came around the net post. "We already won the first set, six–love, and

141

we're ahead, two to one, now.''

"We lost," Gregory said mournfully.

"We haven't lost yet," I told Greg. "Come on, I know we can do better.''

I wasn't too happy myself, because I'd had it all planned that we were going to win all eight points for our team. Then I looked over at Jeff serving and just about split my sides. His serve always did that to me: He winds up for about five minutes and then just poofs the ball in. So I felt more cheerful. We could still win six points.

I doubt if Gregory will ever be famous for his cocky attitude, but he played better after that, and thanks to a little choking on our opponents' part, we tied them at 6–all. Then Greg and I fought off several set points and managed to win the tie breaker. At least we got one set.

"Those two points could decide the whole match," I told Gregory, although I personally doubted it. The grapevine report, from court to court, was that most of the singles matches were going to Hilltop. So we needed *all* our doubles points.

"You can beat their number two team," Jimmy told us. "Good luck!"

"We should've beaten this team," I grumbled. "You and Jeff won't have any trouble."

"We're not counting any chickens," Jimmy said, and he wasn't laughing. Even Jeff wasn't laughing. When you play for your team, you don't fool around.

142

We got off to a bad start in our second match, when they led, 2–1, and then, after a long, stubborn battle, Greg lost his serve. In doubles, a set can be decided by one service break. Greg knew it, and he was crushed.

"Don't worry. We'll break back," I told him. But it's hard to concentrate when you have to cheer up your partner all the time. So in the next game, trying extra hard to break their serve, I missed two easy volleys. One just caught the tape and dropped back on our side, and the other, on game point, was a put-away that hit the line. However, in an honest mistake, they called it out. It was 4–1 for them, my serve.

"Four-one is just one service break," I told Greg, and he started playing better. But then I got to thinking about his playing better and my playing worse, so naturally I played badly and almost lost my serve.

"Hit the ball in the court," I muttered to myself, "and quit worrying."

I did win my serve, finally, and from then on, I remembered Coach's advice to let them make the errors. They did, and we won the next four games for 6–4, first set!

We were going great and forged ahead 3–1 in the second set. The rest of our team were finished with their matches, and they all came over to watch us. All the Hilltop guys were watching, too.

"Come on, Dori! Come on, Greg!" our team were

143

all shouting. Our coach was shushing them up, but one of the Hilltop guys yelled, "Come on, *team*. We *gotta* have this set!"

So—the whole match depended on us.

Greg froze, and before we knew it, the score evened up at 3–3. Then a funny thing happened to me. Suddenly I couldn't miss. The more they watched, and the louder they yelled, the better I played. It was kind of like being in a play on a stage. It wasn't me making those shots; it was the character in the play.

With Hilltop serving at 3–all, though, Greg still couldn't return a serve. I kept saving their ad to give him another chance, but the harder he tried to make it, the worse he missed it. I know the feeling, when you're trying too hard.

"I'm sorry," he said about fifteen times. "Give me one more chance. I'll get it back next time." And finally he did. It was our ad.

Now, don't press, I told myself. *Just get it back.* But it wasn't that easy. I returned serve with my best cross-court chip. It landed in their alley, nice and short, but Hilltop's server managed to return it off the rim of his racket! It was a crazy wood shot that hit the net and bounced over me. Greg raced over behind me and stabbed it back! The Hilltop team was so surprised that they just stood there with their mouths open.

I grinned at Greg and said, "Nice work!"

144

"Aw, you won the game, saving all those ads," he told me.

"I can't win it all by myself," I said. "We're a *team.*"

Dad always says that it's very important to encourage your partner in doubles, and we won the next two games in no time. We'd won both sets, and four more points for our team!

Then they told us. Jimmy and Jeff had won all their sets for eight points. Larry, Harry, Carlos, and Maria had each won one set in singles, for four points, and Greg and I had won six. So it was Rock Canyon 18, Hilltop 14. We'd *all* won it!

"Even with girls you beat us," the Hilltop coach said, when he and our coach shook hands.

"That's what did it," Coach Hannigan told him.

Wow! Can you believe that?

13 • A CHAMPION—AND
A RUNNER-UP

"I wish I could go on a diet that'd make me stop growing taller," I grumbled.

"Don't worry," Mom said. "Girls don't grow much after they're fourteen."

"And it's good for your serve," Grandma said.

Mom cut our hair short, Betsy's and mine. "There," she said, snapping her scissors, "isn't that nice? It turned out curly."

"I look like something that came out of Dr. Seuss," I snorted.

Everybody calls Betsy and me "those redheaded Sinclair girls," and says we look *so* much alike. We may look alike, but we sure are different. I'd been working on Betsy's tennis, to get her ready for Santa Monica. It was her first tournament, and she wasn't a bit nervous, even the day before it started.

"When do I get my butterflies?" she wanted to know.

She can get the ball back as long as I hit it near her, but I don't have that much patience. Once we got up to a hundred, and I couldn't help it—I ran up to net and smashed her nice high ball to her backhand corner. She swung so hard, with both hands on her racket, the way the little kids hold it, that she spun around in a circle, and I was sorry I'd made her miss. Maybe we could have set a new world record!

It's kind of fun to be a teacher, though. It makes me feel great when she says, "Oh! *I* see." When Betsy was six, she couldn't hit anything. Now her backhand is just as steady as her forehand. Stacy and Dave had lessons with the best pros Dad could afford. I have Grandma, and Betsy only has me.

"Okay, we'll win anyway," I told her.

Grandma told me it does me good to go over the basics with Betsy. Then I won't forget them myself. Like, "Get your racket back. Have it ready before the ball comes. Then all you have to do is move forward and hit through the ball. That way you put all your weight into your shots instead of having to jerk the racket back *and* forward."

"Like laying your bat back?" Betsy asked, and I

147

said, "Exactly. And always go back to the center of the baseline after you hit your drive. Be ready for the next one." That's another thing you have to keep reminding yourself of. It gets to be automatic after a couple thousand times.

Betsy doesn't get mad like I did when Davy was telling me what to do. She just keeps trying.

Another thing we work on is footwork. It's kind of like dancing, and some people take ballet to help their tennis. You're supposed to take three little light steps instead of one big clodhopper, for instance, or five little ones instead of going one-two-*clump*. When you have to run a long way for the ball, the little steps help you not to land on the wrong foot for hitting your forehand or backhand. But the important thing is to get there, no matter which foot you land on. The *most* important thing is to win the point.

"Keep on your toes!" I called, when Betsy was receiving my serve. "Don't just stand there."

"Okay. Like this?" Betsy said, dancing up and down. That's a good way for little kids to do it. I even jump up and down myself sometimes, if I'm getting lazy, to make me feel more peppy.

Sometimes I get impatient when Betsy can't do what I tell her to do. I thought she'd never learn how to serve. But I try not to be impatient, because I don't want her to get discouraged. "Just try to get your *first* serve in the court, even if you do have two

148

MATCH POINT

chances,'' I told her. ''It doesn't have to be all that great—don't waste it.'' I'd heard the Davis Cup captain telling that to his team before they beat Mexico. It was on TV. So if that's what the big stars are supposed to do, it's good enough for Betsy.

''Wait till Dad sees how you can play now,'' I told her the day before we went to Santa Monica. ''Maybe you'll even win the Ten and Unders, and will he be surprised!'' There are some awfully good ten-year-olds, though, so I didn't really think she would. But she'd had a lot earlier start than I'd had, and I was planning to win the Fourteens.

The next day, when we got to the Santa Monica tennis center at Lincoln Park, I looked all over for Shelby. And she was looking for me. We found each other in the ladies' room.

''Dori, your hair!'' she squealed. ''I *like* it.'' She always makes everything sound so wonderful; she's really fun to have for a friend.

''Well, I'm getting used to it,'' I admitted.

We couldn't play doubles together in this tournament, because it's an interscholastic. You have to play with someone from your own school. I was playing Fourteen singles, and doubles with Jimmy. Jimmy was playing Sixteen singles, his first tournament. Shelby was playing singles and doubles for her school—*they* have a girls' team. And Betsy got to play in the special younger girls' division.

149

MATCH POINT

We had a great time the first few days. The tournament center is at Lincoln Park, a few blocks from the ocean, and we all stayed in the same motel, which is practically on the beach. April is still too cold for swimming, but we played some volleyball and had races on the hard sand and listened to the surf. The weatherman was predicting a storm, and there were some really big waves.

Mom took off work to drive us up and stay with us. Dad couldn't get off, and besides, he said he'd had it with the hassles of junior tennis. Every day we played singles in the morning and doubles in the afternoon, and every evening we went out on the town to celebrate. All of us were winning—Jimmy, me, Shelby, and Betsy, too. We ate at an elegant cafeteria, played table tennis in the rec room at Lincoln Park, and, the second night, went to see a movie. It was a Disney show. It wasn't the funniest one I've ever seen, but we couldn't stop laughing, anyway, even after we got back to the motel.

"Quick! Follow that crazy *dawg*," Shelby drawled, and Jimmy and Betsy and I burst out laughing all over again.

We got to bed early. We wanted to win again.

Unfortunately, the top doubles team from Rock Canyon High is not one of the best in southern California. Jimmy and I *lucked* out for three days, and then got *wiped* out. Jimmy lost his singles, too, and Shelby lost *her* singles and doubles. So who did

150

she lose her singles to? Luellen!

"We got sent off to a high school court without even an umpire," she told us. "I never had a chance." Then she grinned. "I have to admit I couldn't have beaten her, anyway. But you will, Dori."

"You'd better believe it," I said fervently.

There wouldn't be any excuse for me if I didn't, I figured, because this time she was on the other side of the draw, so we'd be playing in the finals—if we both got there. We'd have an umpire and linesitters and ball boys—the works.

When I first looked at the draw, I said, "Oh, no!" I'd drawn a bye in the first round (that means you don't have to play anybody till the second round); then I'd probably play Jackie Van Arsdale. In the third round, I'd probably have to play the top-seeded player, Janice Kristal. She's ranked number one in southern Cal, and she's a lefty! I'd never played a left-handed player before.

"So? You have to beat her *some*time," I told myself.

The match with Jackie was a surprise.

"Hi," she said happily, when she met me on the court. No father in sight.

"What happened at Long Beach?" I asked her. "Did you get sick or something? When you had to default?"

"No. I just told my father that I wasn't going to
151

play any more tennis unless he stayed home. He wouldn't, so I quit. I guess I made my point, though, because this time I'm on my own."

"That's great," I told her.

She played a lot better without him, too. Luckily I'd improved considerably myself, and after a long battle, I came through 4–6, 7–5, 6–3.

"You're looking good," she said, when she came up to the net to shake hands. "Good luck in your next round."

"Thanks a lot," I said. "I was lucky in *this* round."

I invited her to stay at our house if she came to La Jolla in July. Mom had said I could.

Mom was having problems trying to watch Betsy and me at the same time. That little kid was plowing right through the competition, including the ten-year-olds! There weren't as many kids in the Ten and Unders as in the Fourteens, though, so after she won her match the day I played Jackie, she was in the semifinals.

On Thursday, I played Janice Kristal, and I had a good rooting section. The Tens skipped a day, so Betsy was watching with Mom, Shelby, and Jimmy.

"I have to catch the Greyhound right after, but I wouldn't miss this match," he told me. He couldn't stay any longer, because he ran out of money.

"You sure did great in your first tournament," I told him. "Specially having to play in the Sixteens."

152

His birthday just missed the date for Fourteen and Under. I'd thought he was older than that, because he's in some of Davy's classes, but he's in an independent study program that lets him advance as fast as he can. I wish I could do that, but I'm not that smart.

Janice is a very nice girl, as Shelby'd said. She's a little taller than I am, and she has dark brown eyes and hair that's cut in straight bangs and rolled under at her shoulders. She wears dark-rimmed glasses, and she's very serious about her tennis.

Talk about concentration! Even in the warm-up rally, she never took her eyes off the ball. She must have climbed out of her playpen onto the court, or maybe they hung tennis balls for a mobile on her crib.

Then we started playing, and what a serve! Did you ever try to return a left-handed American twist? It hops the wrong way, just the way you don't expect it when you're used to a right-handed serve.

So? It bounced crooked to the right, I told myself. *I'll get it next time.*

Then she served in the ad court, only she used a slice serve to my backhand, and it bounced way off to my left and ran me off the court. It was hard to hit a forehand *or* a backhand drive off those twisty serves.

Just keep trying, I told myself. *Figure it out.*

I hung on to my own serve, which was going great

153

for a change, and the games went to 6–all. The set had to be decided by a tie breaker, and the way it worked out, Janice got the extra serve on sudden death. It was a server's battle right up to the last point, with me trying to get on top of that crazy-hopping serve. Then, at set point, I got it back!

Janice was serving into the ad court, and instead of hanging back, I moved in toward the ball and hit it early, on the rise. She stayed back, so I made a good solid shot, not trying to kill it, and went in to net to volley her return. She should have lobbed, but she went for a hard, down-the-line passing shot that just ticked the top of the net and dropped—on her side.

My gallery almost fell off their bench clapping, and I had the first set. Janice looked more determined than ever, but once I got that serve figured out, I was feeling so good that I couldn't miss anything. My timing was fantastic. It had never been that good before. I felt like I was somebody else, not me, Dori Sinclair.

And I won in straight sets. I was the dark horse, upsetting the champion!

I could have flown three feet over the net, but I just ran up and shook hands.

"Congratulations," Janice said. "You played great."

After my match with Janice, the semifinals on Friday seemed easy. I won, 6–2, 6–3, and made the finals. Since I finished my match long before Betsy finished her semis, I went with Mom and Shelby to watch her.

Betsy was playing a cute little Japanese girl, whose mom told us she was only seven years old. Mayumi (that's *My Yoomy)* twinkled around the court in her teeny tennis shoes, whaling every ball, both hands gripping the cutoff handle of a full-size racket. The score was a set apiece when we got there, and it seemed like every point lasted about five minutes. Betsy was so tired that she just stood in the middle of her baseline. She moved around only when she had to, and she barely got Mayumi's terrific drives back. With longer legs and more weight behind those shots, Mayumi could have put them away.

"She's got beautiful groundstrokes," Mom told her mother, who was sitting near us. Ms. Yukimura just beamed and nodded her head. It was past dinner time, so, except for us, no one was there. People don't go all out to watch the Ten and Unders.

I hoped I wouldn't get a crick in my neck, turning my head back and forth to watch those long points. Of course, I was rooting for Betsy, but sometimes I couldn't help kicking my foot to help Mayumi's great drives go over the net.

Wow! She was so good!

I'm still amazed at Betsy, even though she's getting to be a winner: She's so calm all the time. I don't think she'll ever have butterflies in her stomach.

Finally, the immovable object prevailed over the

155

irresistible force. Mayumi ran herself out of breath and missed a couple of shots, and suddenly it was over, 7–5, in the third.

Mayumi could hardly reach over the net to shake hands, and she didn't say a word, but she was beaming, just like her mother. Betsy was crying!

"I wish I didn't beat her," she said. "She's such a nice little girl."

I think Betsy expected the match to go on forever. She was still sniffling when we went out to dinner.

Mom gave her a hug. "Tell you what," she said. "Would you like to invite Mayumi to stay with us for the next tournament? Maybe you could even play doubles together."

The day of the finals was so gray that we couldn't see the beach from the motel. We had breakfast and went to Lincoln Park early, before almost anybody else was there. The wind was blowing through the tall old eucalyptus trees, scattering bits of trash across the courts.

Oh, no, I thought. *I can't play in this wind!*

Betsy's match started at ten, on the court next to the grandstand court, and mine was at eleven. Mom watched Betsy, but I was too nervous. Shelby offered to hit with me, to get me warmed up, on an empty court, but somebody took the court away from us, so we went to the rec room and played cards.

I didn't know, until it was time for me to go out on

156

the grandstand court for my match, that Dad was
there! He'd come to see the finals. "Hey, how about
that?" he said. "*Two* of my girls in the finals." Betsy was still playing, but she waved at him.

"We wanted to surprise you," Mom told me.

They'd surprised me all right. I wished Dad hadn't
come. What if I played badly? What if I lost?

The number one court at Lincoln Park has a tier of
benches along one side and a covered grandstand,
with chairs in it, at one end. Dad and Mom sat there,
so that they could look over at the next court and see
Betsy's match and watch me at the same time. Little
kids' matches go on and on. Maybe my match would
be all over before Betsy's was. Maybe Luellen would
smash me, 0 and 0.

The wind was roaring louder every minute. I kept
wishing we would start, but Luellen was late. Not
late enough for them to default her—just ten minutes, enough for me to get the shivers. All I had was a
light sweater over my tennis dress, and my legs were
turning purple.

Luellen arrived in a pink warmup jacket and long
pants. She carried a fancy case and three rackets. Her
blond hair was pulled back to the top of her head and
tied with a pink bow, and she was wearing those gold
earrings again. And a locket. I don't see how anyone
can wear all that stuff when she's playing tennis, but
I guess even lots of the stars do.

Finals matches aren't much like the earlier ones

157

you have on back courts, or the ones at a high school. All of a sudden, everybody wants to watch you play, when nobody but your mother ever did before. There's an important official in the high umpire's chair, testing the public address system; ball boys (or girls); linesitters for baselines, sidelines, and even the center service line; and a top junior to call the serves.

Luellen waved at him and said, "Hi, Ted. Are you going back East this summer?" I have to admit that it would be hard to find somebody she doesn't know.

After our warmup rally, Luellen took off her jacket and pants. Her dress was pink, too. My teeth were still chattering, so I kept my sweater on.

"Players ready? Linesitters ready? Play!" called the umpire into the microphone.

Luellen had won the toss but chose to let me serve first. That way, she could choose the side she wanted to start on. The way that wind was blowing, I didn't know which side was better! She had another reason, and when I started to serve, I found out what it was.

She wanted to break my serve. She almost did, too! My first toss blew back about a foot behind my head! I caught it and tossed again. You can throw the ball up as many times as you want to, as long as you don't touch it with your racket. But after two tosses I didn't want to look ridiculous, so I went ahead and served—into the net. It was a long game, but in spite of two double faults, I won it. I was determined.

When we changed courts, I found myself facing

the grandstand where Dad was sitting. Of course, he didn't wave or anything, but I couldn't help thinking about his watching me play so poorly. I wished he had sat on the side. It didn't bother me about Mom being there. She knew I could play better.

Luellen tossed the ball about six times before her first serve. She took her time. She must have figured out the wind, because after that, she got her first serve in the court every time and took the game without losing a point. I hit her last serve about six feet past the baseline, and it bounced up into the grandstand. Dad threw it back.

"How can I play so badly?" I asked myself. "I can't hit *anything.*"

Then I lost my serve, and Luellen won hers again, and it was 1–3 in games.

"This is ridiculous," I told myself. "Concentrate. Watch the ball."

I tried to figure out which way the wind was blowing, so that I could hit harder against the wind and get my returns lower over the net when the wind was behind me, so they wouldn't go out. Grandma had taught me that, one day when it was windy back home. But *this* wind went every which way. I did win three more games, but Luellen won two, to stay ahead of me, 5–4.

At set point, Luellen's ad, she came to net on her serve. I had the choice of a lob or a passing shot, and I chose the lob. I'd rather have drilled it past her, but

159

I could hit my lobs real hard against the wind, and they wouldn't go out, so I did that and won the point.

"The score is deuce," announced the umpire.

I returned her next serve with another good lob, and it was my ad. If I could win the next point, we'd be all tied up in games at 5–5, first set. I was really concentrating.

Luellen hung back in midcourt, expecting another lob that she could reach up and smash away. So I drilled a passing shot down the line on her forehand side. I couldn't believe what happened! My drive went past Luellen, *but the wind was blowing so hard against it that she went back and got it!* I couldn't reach her neat little drop shot, just over the net, and the score was deuce again. I'd missed my chance.

"That darn wind," I muttered and socked another lob as hard as I could against it. Only all of a sudden the wind wasn't there! My ball sailed a mile out, and I just stood there while Luellen won her next serve, the set point. I was so disgusted that at first I couldn't move. Then I blew up.

"I can't play tennis in this wind!" I ripped out, and I threw my racket way up into the sky. Everybody heard me. I was so ashamed that I wanted to sink through the court, but there we were, just me and Luellen, with everybody watching us. *She* looked like a pink angel.

I caught my racket, so it didn't hit the cement and

160

split. Good thing. I only have one racket.

If the wind bothered Luellen, she never let on. After she won the first game of the second set, breaking my serve, we passed each other at the net post, changing courts.

"Tough break on that passing shot," she said, too kindly. I didn't say anything. I didn't trust myself.

The next time we passed at the net post, the umpire was announcing, "Game to Ms. Jarvis. She leads three games to love, second set, having won the first set, six games to four."

"It takes a lot of experience to play in the wind," Luellen said, with that sweet smile. "I know you can play better."

I felt like yanking off that pretty pink hair ribbon. What I should have done was stick to my tennis and beat her.

But I didn't. All I could think of was how I'd disgraced myself in front of all those people. Including Dad. I wasn't only a bad player. I was a bad sport.

After the match, at the awards ceremony, I got a trophy. The Runner-up. And Betsy had won the Ten and Unders.

I wanted to be glad, but I was jealous. Dad got his surprise all right, but it was Betsy. And she only won because she never gets bothered by anything. Mom told us that the little girl Betsy had played ended up sitting down on the court, bawling, because her shots blew out. I was just as bad, and I'm fourteen.

"It wasn't the wind that beat you," Dad told me. "It was your concentration. You beat yourself." He didn't act mad at me or anything, but I'd wanted him to be *proud*.

On the way home in the station wagon, they were all up front singing, Mom and Dad and Betsy. Dad had flown up so that he could drive us back. But I couldn't have sung even if I'd wanted to. My throat was sore from trying not to cry. I wanted to play the match all over again, so that I could play better. I wouldn't even care if I didn't win. I wanted to say I was sorry that I had acted so badly, but nobody gave me a chance.

"Wait till Stacy and Dave see what we're bringing home," Dad said. "A champion!"

Yeah, and a runner-up.

I almost threw my trophy out the window. I would have, only they charge you five hundred dollars for throwing trash onto the freeway.

14 • I CHALLENGE DAD

Davy sprang a surprise on our family by deciding to enter the interscholastic singles at Ojai in May. He also invited Jimmy to play doubles with him for Rock Canyon High.

Jimmy was nice enough to ask if that was okay with me. He would have been pretty unhappy if I'd said no.

"Sure, go ahead," I told him. *"I'm* not going."

I was too depressed.

Dad found out, a few days after the deadline, and got mad at me. "You didn't enter Ojai?" he demanded. "Why not?"

I didn't know he cared what I did. I thought he'd be so happy about Davy that he wouldn't even notice.

"I didn't want to," I muttered.

"You beat the top-seeded player at Santa Monica, and you don't want to go to Ojai?" Dad shook his head the way he does when he can't understand us kids.

"How did you know I beat Janice?" I asked. "You weren't there."

"Your mother told me all about it," he said.

Fathers are funny. Just when you think they're about to kill you, they do something nice.

"Well, since you're not going up there, why don't you drive out to La Jolla with me this weekend?" he said.

I couldn't believe it. Just Dad and me. We didn't even take Betsy. He told me to wear my tennis clothes and bring my racket, and when we got to La Jolla, we didn't go to the public courts. He drove into the La Jolla Beach and Tennis Club! You have to be a member to play there, unless you're a top junior like Stacy was, or Dave. Sometimes they got invited to play exhibitions.

It's a superbeautiful clubhouse, with apartments right on the seashore, and tall palms and a lagoon and flowers all over the place. It's also superexpensive. So is their pro, Mr. McIver, but that's what Dad was taking me there for: a lesson! He'd made

165

special arrangements because, he said, *I* was getting to be a top junior.

"Gol-lee!" I whispered when Dad walked out on the lesson court and introduced me to Mr. McIver. He's real tall, with silver hair and a nice smile. He used to be a national doubles champion, and he'd been high up in the singles, too.

"Another Sinclair?" he asked, looking me over.

I figured I must be dreaming. Even when he sent me to the baseline and started feeding me balls, I still couldn't believe it.

"I'd like to get an idea of your strengths and weaknesses today, Dori," he said, "so we'll know what to work on."

I was going to have more lessons? I looked at Dad, and he was trying to act like nothing was happening, but he had this sneaky little grin. After we rallied a while, Mr. McIver said, "Dori has sound ground-strokes and a strong serve for her age. I don't think we'll change anything right now." Then he said, "Come up to net, and let's see your volley."

He fed me another basketful of balls, reminding me not to swing but just reach out and punch the ball. "Remember, no matter where you are on the court, don't let the ball get so close to your body that your stroke is cramped," he told me.

After my lesson, he had a talk with Dad, and I heard him say, "This kid has a better forehand than—" I didn't hear who, and Dad wouldn't tell me, no matter how much I teased.

Driving home, Dad and I had a really nice talk. I thanked him for my lessons, and he said, "You've come a long way all by yourself, Dori."

"How come you're being so nice to me," I asked, "when I played so badly at Santa Monica and even threw my racket?"

"I used to throw my racket," Dad said. He was paying attention to his driving, and looking straight ahead. For a minute or so, he didn't say anything, and his mouth was clamped shut, so I could tell that he was really serious. "One day, I slung it across the court after I missed a setup, and it hit one of the ball boys."

Gol-lee! My dad threw his racket and hit somebody?

"Did he get hurt?" I asked.

"Enough to make me hold on to my racket for a long time," he said.

"I'll never throw it again," I promised.

"Unfortunately," Dad said, "losing your temper is not something you can promise not to do. Especially for us redheads."

"People with red hair don't all have tempers," I said. "Betsy doesn't."

"That's true," Dad said. "Besides, it's only a myth that redheads get angry faster than people who don't have red hair, but I'm afraid that you and I are stuck with our tempers, anyway."

167

I've never had a talk like that with Dad before. It was really great. When we were almost home, I pestered him again to tell me what Mr. McIver said.

"Who doesn't have as good a forehand as I do?" I begged. But he wouldn't tell; he just laughed at me.

I felt really close to Dad then, but it didn't last very long. When we got home, Mom was kneeling on the living room carpet with pins in her mouth, fitting Stacy's wedding gown. It was white lace over pale blue satin. Stacy looked so beautiful that I got tears in my eyes.

Dad doesn't want Stacy to get married. He thinks she's too young. "Sam can't support her till he gets his D.D.S.," he says, and Stacy says *she* can make plenty of money teaching tennis.

Dad and Sam both get mad when she says that!

"You could make more playing the circuit or in World Team Tennis," Dad says. (Los Angeles had already drafted her for their team, but Stace had said no, she couldn't leave Sam.)

"I can support you. I can get a job and still take courses," Sam says, and Stacy says, "That way, you'll never get through. I might as well teach and get *some* use out of my tennis."

She says that as though tennis is just a big pain, and I know how Dad feels: After all that work—we were so proud of her when she'd won the Nationals and got invited to Wimbledon—to just throw it away! It doesn't seem fair, somehow.

168

"Why don't you go to Wimbledon and *then* get married?" Dad keeps asking her. "What's the big rush?"

It's because Sam is getting out of college for summer vacation, and Stace wants to go on a honeymoon in Europe. She and Sam argue about that all the time, too.

"If I'd play in the European tournaments, they'd pay our expenses and give us housing," Stacy told Sam yesterday. "And we ought to travel before we have a baby."

"A baby!" Sam exclaimed. "You know we can't have a baby till I get my degree. And we're not going to Europe till *I* can pay for it."

"Chauvinist," Stacy said scornfully.

If they're going to fight so much before they get married, they'd better not get married. That's what Dad thinks, too. So when he saw Stace in the living room, the arguments started all over again.

When our family gets into arguments, Mom is the one who always calms us down. But Mom was so busy with the wedding that she was getting pretty uptight herself. "You don't know what it's like being the mother of the bride! I have to do *everything*," she snapped. "And the wedding's only three weeks away!"

Then Davy came slamming into the house and went to his room. He'd just got back from Ojai. I looked at Dad, and he looked like he was thinking just what

169

I was: How come Davy didn't come into the living room and tell us that he'd won? He always wins. . . .

Davy didn't come out of his room. When Dad finally went and knocked on his door, Davy wouldn't open it. He called out, "Okay, so I lost. I don't want to talk about it." Dad went to *his* room, and it was pretty gloomy around our house for a long time.

But a really neat thing happened to me at school that week, so *I* wasn't gloomy. We had our annual awards assembly on Friday, the first of June, and I got my first varsity letter. I also got Most Valuable Player!

I could hardly wait to tell Dad, but I saved it for a surprise when he took me to La Jolla for my second lesson. I'd been afraid Dad was going to forget about the lesson, but he didn't.

"Our team won the county championship this year," I told him. "We beat all the other teams in our league."

"Oh, yes, the bush league," Dad said, and it made me kind of mad, but I figured he was just teasing me.

"I thought Jimmy would get Most Valuable Player, since he's the captain. But the guys all voted for *me,* and Jimmy said I deserved it, too."

"That's one big step for womankind," Dad joked, but he still didn't sound very happy. He couldn't get his mind off Stace and Davy.

I had a good lesson. When we were working on my volley, Mr. McIver stopped and asked, "You really

170

like coming to net, don't you, Dori?"

"I like to get the point over with," I admitted. "Is that okay?"

"It's unusual for a girl your age to be so aggressive," he told me, "but as long as you build up to it with good approach shots, it certainly is okay. It gives you a big advantage, getting the ball back that much sooner, so that your opponent doesn't have time to prepare her shot. That was Billie Jean's game, and she dominated women's tennis for years."

"Dori is on the boys' team at her school," Dad said, from the net post where he was watching.

"It isn't a boys' team," I said. "It's the only one we have."

"She even beat out the team captain for the Most Valuable Player award," Dad told him. Boy, did it feel good to have my father bragging about *me*, for a change!

"Our team won the league championship," I told Mr. McIver, and he made a big O with his thumb and finger. He was feeding me overheads, so that he could look at my smash, when Dad added, "Of course it was only high school tennis, out in the boondogs."

High school tennis! Boy, was I furious! I reached up and smashed the next ball as hard as I could. It hit the basket, knocked it over, and bounced over the fence into the next court. Yellow balls were rolling all over, and the old guy in the next court came to the

171

fence and bawled me out for disrupting his match.

I wouldn't talk to my father all the way home, and after telling me that there'd be no more lessons if I ever acted like that again, he didn't talk to me either. He'd been right about one thing. You can't promise not to lose your temper. I hadn't meant to do what I did, but I wasn't about to say I was sorry. *He* ought to have been sorry! He'd been nice enough about Jimmy, but he didn't have to be so snooty about our high school tennis.

"I bet I could beat *you*," I muttered.

We were stopped at a red light, and Dad looked down at me like he thought I was crazy. Then he burst out laughing. It was the first time he'd laughed since Davy lost at Ojai, and it sounded kind of nice.

"You're on," he said. And then he said, "I'm sorry, Dori. You've done a great job on your tennis, and I'm sure the team play helped. McIver said you have a better forehand than Stacy."

"*Stacy*," I squealed. Wow!

I didn't think Dad would really play with me, but on Monday morning, he hauled me out of bed when it was practically still dark and said, "Hurry up and get dressed. We have time for a set or so before I go to work."

I don't know where I got the idea that I could beat him. When I get mad I'll say anything. But Stacy could beat him, and Mr. McIver thinks I have a better forehand than hers. Besides, even if I was just a

172

boondogs high school player, I'd upset the number one Fourteen and Under in southern California, even if I hadn't beat Luellen. So I figured I could at least give Dad *some* competition.

"You want to go to the high school courts or the club?" Dad asked me.

"High school," I said. It was closer, so we could play longer.

Nobody else was around. I kind of wished Jimmy was there to see me getting to play with my dad. He opened a can of brand new balls and let me choose which side I wanted to rally on.

We rallied for about five minutes, and then Dad said, "Ready?"

"Sure," I said. "Spin for serve?"

Dad spun his racket, and I won, so I served first. "Take all the practice serves you want," Dad said, so I took a bunch of them. I was so nervous that I couldn't get even one in.

I decided that I'd just start anyway. When you're playing, you *have* to get them in, but it's a good idea to loosen up first.

Get that first one in, I told myself, and I did. It wasn't much, and Dad should have killed it, but he just hit it back—to my forehand! That made me kind of mad, because I could tell that he wasn't really trying. So I drilled a down-the-line to his backhand, ran in, and put his weak return away.

"Great volley," Dad said.

"Anybody could do that," I muttered to myself. "He'd better try, too, or he'll be sorry."

I got ahead, 40–love, and then I got to brooding over how he was going easy on me—and served a double fault. On the next two points, I made errors, and it was deuce.

Concentrate, you dope, I told myself. *If he wants to lose, let him. You don't have to beat yourself!* I sliced a good serve down the center line and ran in, but he hit his return into the net, so I had the ad.

"Great serve," Dad said.

"Who's he rooting for, himself or me?" I grumbled, but then I took a deep breath and concentrated on my next serve. It wasn't much, so I stayed back, and Dad hit his return to my forehand again. We had a long rally, cross-courts and down-the-lines, with me furnishing all the power and Dad just standing on the baseline getting the ball back, till I got so mad that I hit a screaming cross-court placement that caught him going the wrong way.

"Great shot!" Dad said. "Good game."

We changed courts, and it was his serve. I wasn't too surprised when the first one came in easy. I made a pretty good return, but even playing at half speed, Dad is tough, and he began hitting every ball to my backhand instead of my forehand. Mr. McIver had said that I have "a good defensive backhand, but it needs work." Dad sure was working it, but I won the game, and it was 2–0 for me. He figured he could win

174

a game anytime he wanted to, I guessed.

I won my serve again, so it was 3–0, but then Dad served four straight aces, and it was 3–1. Apparently, though, he decided that I should win my serve again. When it was 40–15, I hit a down-the-line that just missed, but Dad didn't say anything. That *really* made me mad.

"My shot was out," I yelled at him.

"Oh, was it?" he asked innocently.

I walked up to the net. "If you're just going to let me win, we might as well not play," I told him.

"I'm sorry, Dori," Dad agreed. "You're dead right. From now on, watch out!"

So it was 40–30, my serve, and on the next point Dad went all out for deuce. He returned the serve like a bullet to my backhand corner, but I managed to block it back. Dad had been so sure that I couldn't touch it that he missed an easy setup. And he didn't miss it on purpose! I could tell the difference. So it was 4–1 for me.

It was a lot more fun when Dad played hard. I had to run all over the court, and my drives went back flatter and faster, because his shots were so powerful. Before, it was hard to concentrate, because I couldn't help thinking that he wasn't trying, but after he started going all out, I didn't have time to think about anything else. I just played tennis.

He won his next service, but I got a lot of his toughest shots back, and it was a long game. He

175

finally won it with an American twist.

"I don't use that serve often," he told me. "It's too hard on my back." So he was really trying.

Serving at 4–2, I knew it was an important game. There'd be a big difference between 5–2, if I won it, and 4–3, with Dad's serve coming up. I lost the first two points, but I figured out why. When I lose points on my serve, it's usually because I'm rushing it. So I took my time, got two first serves in deep, and won the points to even the score at 30–all. That game went to deuce, ad in, ad out, about a hundred times. I got stubborn and refused to lose.

Once, on Dad's ad, I was way back at the baseline from chasing a lob, and he made a dinky little drop shot. I've never run so fast in my life, and when I got there, I drop-shot it back. It ticked the top of the net and rolled over on his side. *Nobody* could have gotten that one back. And then I won the next two points for game.

Dad wasn't saying "great shot" anymore. It was 5–2 for me, and he was looking pretty grim. He bounced the ball a lot of times on the baseline, getting ready to serve. People do that sometimes when they're nervous, but Dad couldn't have been nervous, could he?

For the first time, I thought, *Maybe I can win.* And then I thought, *Oh, no—if I beat him, he'll kill me!*

Dad served a fault and then double-faulted, and I

moved over to the ad court. *Poor Dad,* I was thinking. *Davy lost at Ojai, Stacy won't go to Wimbledon,
. . . I just can't beat him.*

Pow! went his serve, whizzing past me. *Pow! Pow!
Pow!*

The game was over.

I quit feeling sorry for Dad and concentrated on
my serve. If I won it, I had the set. If I lost it, the
score would be 4–5, with Dad serving. The way my
Dad can serve, he'd even it up at 5–all in games, and
there'd go my chance. It would be hard to break his
serve again.

So it's now or never, I thought. *Come on, Boondogs!*

I never played better, and it seemed like the game
lasted longer than all the rest put together. When it
was Dad's ad for the umpteenth time, and he was
crowding the net for a put-away, I socked a lob as
hard as I could to his backhand corner. There was no
way he could reach it, I was sure. But he jumped way
up in the air, kicking his legs like scissors, got his
racket on top of the ball, and smashed it at my feet. I
couldn't do anything.

Then he won his serve again for 5–all.

I was still planning to win, somehow or other, if it
took all day, but Dad came up to the net with his
hand out.

" 'Fraid we'll have to call it quits," he said, "or
I'll be late for work."

177

"Oh, *no,*" I grumbled, but I guessed he had to stop.

"I had no idea you could play that well, Dori," he told me. "I was overconfident at first, and you almost did me in."

I couldn't help grinning. It'd been so much fun playing Dad, even if it had ended up in a tie. "I'll do you in the next time," I told him, and he said, "You're on!"

15 • SINCLAIR VS. JARVIS

One morning near the end of June, Dad, Betsy, and I were sitting at the breakfast bar, and Mom was making pancakes at the stove, when Davy came in the back door, waving the sports section of the Sunday newspaper.

"Rock Canyon Racketeers Make Big Racket," Davy read out loud. "Sinclair Family Racks Up More Trophies."

Dad grabbed the paper and spread it out.

"They must have *racked* their brains on those headlines," he said, and Betsy laughed so hard that she fell off her stool. She likes those corny puns.

Betsy picked herself up, and she was okay, so we all started laughing. Mom flipped a pancake onto the floor, and I was drinking milk at the time, and it squirted up my nose.

We'd known that they were planning to write a story about our family, because the photographer had come to our house and had taken a bunch of extra pictures after the Southern Cal Junior Championships. Davy had practiced a lot to get back on his game after losing at Ojai, and he'd won the Boys' Eighteens. I'd won the Girls' Fourteens—I'll tell you about that later—and though Betsy hadn't won the singles, she and Mayumi had won the little girls' doubles. They were *so* happy; she just loves Mayumi. Betsy didn't mind losing the singles. "I only win when it's *win*dy!" she cracked. She's as bad as Dad.

Jimmy had been there, too, in the Boys' Sixteens, and he'd almost won his semis. Boy, he's going to give Davy trouble some day! I'm so proud of him.

Dad read us the article in the paper. Besides telling about Davy and Betsy and me, it said that Grandma was the United States Senior Women's Fifty-five and Over Clay-court Singles Champion, that Dad and Davy had previously won the National Hard-court Father and Son, and that Stacy, National Girls' Champion for two years in a row, was off on a honeymoon junket to Europe, where she was playing tournaments in Paris, Barcelona, Munich, and Vienna. "Tennis is a great sport for families," it said, and

Dad said, "They can say *that* again."

"What about me?" Mom asked. "Didn't they hear I made Number Two on the 'C' ladder?"

"You have to read the fine print," Dad told her. "It says here that 'Mr. and Mrs. George Sinclair are the Mixed Doubles Champions at the Rock Canyon Racquet Club.' "

"Well, that's more like it," Mom said. "Anybody want more juice? Pancakes?"

"You'd better sit down and eat something yourself," Dad told her. "And wait till you get a load of these pictures!"

There was a page of photos inside, candid shots of all of us holding our rackets in weird positions, with captions to explain why we had our faces all screwed up: BETSY KEEPS EYE ON BALL and DORI DEMONSTRATES FIERCE CONCENTRATION THAT WON HER TOP SPOT IN SOUTHERN CALIFORNIA TOURNEY.

You can't believe everything you read in the newspapers. I'm not Number One; Luellen still outranks me. For three weeks in June, I didn't do anything but practice to beat Luellen. (That's not counting being in Stacy's wedding, which was bee-you-tiful.) Stacy offered to play me for practice before she got married. I couldn't beat her, but we had some close matches. She also told me a lot of stuff that helped my game.

"A champion never misses a setup," she said, and, "The pros play percentage tennis. Somebody figured

181

out that seventy-five percent of the points a player loses are on errors, and only twenty-five percent are on placements.''

Then she told me, "You're going to be better than I am. You have more natural athletic ability.'' I think she figured that Dad wouldn't be so disappointed at her quitting if he had me.

Stace finally got Sam to go to Europe "just this one time.'' Stacy is sort of like Mom. When Dad says no, Mom doesn't argue, but somehow or other, it ends up with Dad saying, "Well, if it means that much to you. . . .'' That's only when it does mean a lot to her, though. Usually we do what Dad wants.

Well, anyway, back to Luellen. I didn't beat her at Southern Cal. Here's what happened: First, my draw was about the worst it could have been. Janice Kristal was seeded first, Luellen second (because even though I'd beaten Janice once, Luellen had beaten me twice), and I was third. I wasn't expecting to be seeded at all. It's the first time I ever was.

So if I made it past the first rounds, with no dark horses beating me, I'd still undoubtedly have to beat Janice before I could play Luellen.

I almost *did* lose in the first round, to Kerry Kendall, who is over a year younger and a head shorter than I am. She was the dark horse when I'd played up at Disneyland two years before. She might have been a dark horse again, but I hung in there when I was down, 2–5, in the second set after losing the first. It wasn't that I was playing so badly, either. She was good!

The rest of the rounds through the quarters were easy, after Kerry, so I made it to the semis. So did Luellen and Janice. I was worried about whether I could upset Janice again; she's really tough. If I didn't beat her, I wouldn't get to play Luellen. I couldn't wait to make up for the time she'd cheated me and for that windy day when I'd played so badly. I *knew* I could beat her.

So what happened? Janice and I had another long service battle, which I won, 7–5, 4–6, 7–5. The same day, Shelby and I had a tough three-set match that put us in the doubles finals. Shelby was ecstatic and wanted to celebrate. All I wanted to do was sack out and rest up for my singles finals with Luellen.

We were staying at a motel in Hollywood, with Shelby's mom for a chaperone. I took a dip in the pool with Shelby and some other kids, and we ate at a really super steak place called Johnny's, and then I made Shelby let me go to bed.

I never thought to ask if Luellen had won her semifinals. She'd drawn Jackie Van Arsdale, who wasn't even seeded. I'd been delighted to hear that Jackie'd made it to the semis, upsetting the fourth-seeded player, but I didn't expect her to get any farther.

When I showed up for my eleven o'clock finals at the Los Angeles Tennis Club, I was all set to beat the pants off Ms. Luellen Jarvis. So who came out on the court? Jackie Van Arsdale! She'd beaten Luellen!

I was so surprised—and disappointed—that Jackie almost beat *me,* too. My dad was there watching, and so was Jackie's. But he didn't do anything dumb. Of course, we had an umpire and everything, so what could he do? But afterward, when Jackie and I had shaken hands and walked off the court together, Mr. Van Arsdale came up and congratulated me. Wow! Jackie'd sure done a good job on her father.

Dad was really happy. After the awards ceremony, when I got my Southern Cal Championship gold medal, they told me that if I was going to the National Girls' Fourteen and Under Championships in Louisiana in August, the Junior Tennis Foundation would be glad to contribute $150 toward my expenses. But I knew that I wouldn't get to go.

"It's a long way, and it'd cost a lot of money," Dad said. Stacy hadn't got to go East till the Sixteens. And Davy was going to Kalamazoo in August for the National Juniors Eighteen and Under in Michigan. But Davy had had to make a choice, too. "I can't spend any more money on your tennis if you're going out for basketball," Dad had told him.

Davy'd thought it over and decided to stick to tennis. It'd really got him when he'd lost at Ojai; he's not the type to quit when he's behind. He wasn't behind anymore, but he wanted to see how he could

184

do in the East. I can understand that!

Dad was still feeling sorry that I couldn't go, even after we got our pictures in the paper. "There are just too many of us Rock Canyon Racketeers," he told me. He was extra nice to me to make up for not being able to let me go. "Maybe next year," he said, and he asked me if I'd like to play in the Father and Daughter at La Jolla.

"With *you?*" I squealed, and he said, "I'm the only father you've got."

"But aren't you going to play with Davy?" I asked.

The La Jolla is a big tournament, with over a thousand entries, so they have to limit people to three events. Dad likes singles best and always plays in the Junior Vets. He and Mom would play in the Husband and Wife, of course, so if he played with me, he'd have to give up the Father and Son. And he could *win* that. Some of the top girls in the Eighteens play with their fathers, and if he played with me, we wouldn't even be seeded.

"I've never played in the Father and Daughter," Dad said. "I'd like to try it."

So we entered. La Jolla is probably the most fun tournament in the world, but I still wished I could go to Louisiana.

I was hoping Luellen would play at La Jolla, and she did. But she entered the Sixteens!

"For practice," she told everybody. "I don't get

185

that much competition in the Fourteens."

"She sure would've gotten some competition from *me,*" I muttered.

It seemed as if I'd never get to play Luellen—until I looked at the draw in the Father and Daughter. The first-seeded team was Lew Jarvis and Luellen.

Dad was standing beside me with his arm across my shoulders. "Uh-oh!" he said. "Lew Jarvis!"

"Is he any good?" I asked.

"It's been my lifelong ambition to beat him in the Junior Vets," Dad said. "So far, I never have."

"Do you think we could get to the finals?" I asked.

Dad knows practically everybody in tennis, and if he doesn't know them, they usually aren't much good, unless they're from the East. It tells on the draw where everybody comes from. Luckily, the Jarvises were in the other half of the draw. Dad said, "I'd say we have a pretty good chance, except for this team from Tennessee. They have some awfully good tennis in Chattanooga. But we'll give it a try."

We won our first round easily. The father was really good, but his daughter was only nine years old and was a beginner. He was a nice young man; he didn't take losing to us too seriously.

"Melissa and I are going to win this thing in five or ten years," he said, "aren't we, honey?"

Melissa just nodded her head. She hadn't said a word the whole time we were playing. *She* was taking

186

it seriously. But when we shook hands at the end of the match, she smiled at us and then said, "Now can we go to the beach, Daddy?"

The second round was sure different. A little old white-haired couple came out onto the court. They both looked older than Grandma, but the lady was the daughter of the man! He had a real tricky little serve that I had a hard time handling. He sliced and chopped and drop-shot all over the place; the lady just lobbed and lobbed. They both chuckled a lot, and we had fun.

When we reached the semis, we met the team from Tennessee, and it got rough. The father was about Dad's age, and the girl knew Stacy. She'd played against her in the Nationals!

There wasn't any chuckling in that match. "Some people take these family events more seriously than Forest Hills," Dad said. The man played about the same as my dad, and after they'd won the first set, 6–4, Dad got me off in a corner of the court for a conference. "I think I've spotted a weakness," he told me. "Let's try hitting hard down the middle of the court and see what happens."

What happened was that they couldn't decide who was going to take the shots, and they got mad at each other! Dad grinned. "The first rule in doubles," he said, "is 'Don't blame your partner.' "

We won the second set, but they pulled themselves together, and the third was a tug of war. I missed

187

some setups, and it looked like we were going to lose. "I'm sorry," I kept saying.

"The second rule in doubles," Dad said, "is 'Don't blame yourself.' "

So I quit apologizing, and after that I played better. We finally won, 6–4, in the third. After we shook hands and walked off the court, Dad said, "We needed a tough match like that for practice for the finals tomorrow. I think we're getting used to each other, don't you?"

Gol-lee! I never thought Dad would be talking to me like that, like I was Mom or somebody!

The next day, Friday, they had all the junior finals. Then, tacked on way at the end of the afternoon, was the Father and Daughter. Up to then, we'd all won; but the event I really wanted to win was the Father and Daughter.

The number one court at La Jolla Playgrounds has bleachers along one side for the spectators, and Dad and I had a great rooting section: Mom, Grandma, Shelby, Betsy and Mayumi, Davy, Jimmy, and most of the guys on my team, for a few. After the match, we were planning to have a beach party, and I sure hoped I'd feel like celebrating after Dad and I got through with Luellen and her dad.

The Jarvises didn't arrive till after the umpire and linesitters were ready, so Dad and I used the additional time for some extra warming up. I was so nervous that I dropped my racket twice, so I was glad

188

when they finally got out on the court.

Luellen, as usual, looked like a model for a tennis magazine. This time she wore a striped pink and white tank top and white shorts, so wouldn't you know that this was the one time that I wore a fancy tennis dress? Her father is tall and lean, the same build as Dad, with silvery-black hair.

"Well, George, we meet again," Mr. Jarvis said. Right away I didn't like him. So he'd always beaten Dad in the Junior Vets. He didn't have to rub it in.

"This time I have some help," Dad told him.

Boy, I sure hoped I'd be a help.

Luellen didn't pay any attention to me, just to Dad. "Your son is a *wonderful* player," she told him. If there were tournaments for butter-uppers, she'd win them all. There isn't anything my father would rather hear.

"I didn't realize you were Lew's daughter when I saw you play at Santa Monica," Dad told her. "You're a fine player yourself."

I almost made the record books for being the first tennis player to throw her racket before the match even started.

The umpire introduced us to the crowd, pointing out that Luellen had won the Girls' Sixteens earlier in the day, while I'd won the Fourteens.

"All the best Sixteen and Unders have gone East already," I muttered.

"What's that?" Dad asked, and I said, "Oh, I was

189

just wishing that we'd get started."

"The Jarvises won the toss and have elected to serve," the umpire continued, and we started to play.

Mr. Jarvis had a powerful serve, but he served differently to me than to Dad. He went easy on me, and that made me madder than I already was. I *like* to return hard serves.

He won his serve, anyway—I was playing terribly because I was mad—and then it was Dad's serve, and *he* went easy on Luellen! I was playing net, and she blasted her return right at me. If I hadn't been so tense, I could have returned it, but I messed it up.

Dad served hard at Mr. Jarvis, but didn't get his first serve in. Mr. Jarvis returned his second serve with a low lob over my head. That fuzzy yellow ball was just like a daisy sitting there waiting to be picked, so I reached up and smashed it . . . into the net.

So Dad was behind, love–30, on his service, and it was my fault.

Dad walked up to the service court for a conference. "It might be a good idea for you to play back," he told me. I felt awful enough, missing those shots. Now he was giving up on me!

"Please let me stay up," I begged. "I'll do better. Really I will."

But of course I didn't. The harder I tried, the worse I messed up, and we lost the game. I should have stayed back, like he'd said. I did play in the backcourt when Dad served after that, and I started to play better. He won the rest of his serves, and I won mine, but it was too late for that set, so we lost it, 6–3.

Dad said, "You know, Dori, that was a good set, once we got started. I think we can do it."

"You *do?*" I said.

"I've played a lot of mixed doubles with your mom," Dad said. "It's a whole different game, and I get the impression that Lew Jarvis hasn't played it much."

I've seen Dad play with Mom. She stands in the back right-hand corner of the court and returns all the balls that come right to her . . . if she can. Dad covers about three-quarters of the backcourt and runs up to net if there's a short ball. He's a real fast runner.

"Do you want me to play like *Mom?*" I protested.

"Do you want to win?" Dad asked.

So we did it his way the second set, and Luellen never knew what hit her. To win in mixed doubles, Dad said, you can't be a gentleman. After we got ahead, 4–1, Mr. Jarvis started drilling all his shots at me, but I was so glad to get a chance to hit for a change that I got a lot of them back, and it was fun. We won the second set, 6–3. Mom calls this "male chauvinist doubles," but she doesn't mind, and I'd do anything to beat Luellen and her dad, for my dad.

The third set was tougher. Mr. Jarvis caught on

fast, and I'd never played against anyone who hit that hard. But I hung in there and returned every shot I could, till it was 5-all.

Luellen was serving, with my serve coming up next; in spite of our dads taking all those balls, the whole match could depend on us girls. If Dad and I could take her serve and win mine, that would be it. Or vice versa. I wouldn't think about that. "Confidence wins a lot of matches," Grandma always says.

I returned Luellen's first serve cross-court to her corner, and she hit it back cross-court to me. Dad leaped in front of me and walloped a topspin forehand that bounced deep in her alley and took off sideways. Luellen missed it, and she fell over backward.

The gallery went, "Ohhhh," and Mr. Jarvis ran over to help her up. Dad went up to the net, looking worried.

I wasn't worried. "It's a wonder she didn't think up something like that before," I sniffed. "She was probably just saving it for the crucial moment."

Nobody heard me, of course, and Luellen got up and started hobbling around, like she was testing her ankle. Then she limped back to the baseline to serve the second point, and the gallery clapped.

She was serving to Dad, in the ad court, and she just plopped it in, but he was so shook up that he hit it into the net, and it was 15-all. Then she limped

192

back and served to me again. I socked it back as hard as I could, right at her. She didn't fool me. I won the point, but Luellen leaned over and began rubbing her ankle. Her dad walked over, and they had a little talk. Then she served to Dad.

Poor Dad. He couldn't hit hard at Luellen at a time like that, so he hit to Mr. Jarvis, and Mr. Jarvis blasted it past me for the point. I considered falling over and decided against it. I had to keep on my toes and win my point till Dad could pull himself together. I also considered telling Dad that Luellen is noted for being a fake, but he'd never have believed me. *What can I do?* I asked myself. *We can't, we just can't lose this match!*

Luellen was still acting like she couldn't run. She put in another easy serve, so I hit a dinky little drop-shot that landed on her side of the court. She dashed in and got it—and put it away! That's the trouble with dropshots: If your opponent is able to reach them, you're dead. So the score was 40–30, and she was serving to Dad—who drop-shot, too!

The ball dropped on Luellen's side, good and short. Mr. Jarvis and Luellen both raced in to get it, and they got in each other's way. They couldn't have reached it, anyway. It was too good.

So the score went back to deuce. Mr. Jarvis had a talk with Luellen. He seemed kind of mad.

My dad stood his racket up on the handle and pretended to sit on it. He grinned at me. "The little

194

lady seems to have recovered," he told me. "All of a sudden she can run."

After that, we both felt so good that we won the next two points for 6-5, with my serve coming up.

Then we won my serve.

"Game, set, and match to George Sinclair and Dori," announced the umpire, and the whole gallery whistled and cheered.

We shook hands politely with the Jarvises, and Luellen acted like she didn't care. "Are you going to the Nationals, Dori?" she asked me. "It's going to be so much fun."

Dad and I got away from there as fast as we could. I wished I could beat her in the Nationals, but at least we'd won the Father and Daughter. Dad and I are a good team.

"Hot dog!" Dad said. "Hot diggety dog! We beat them!"

16 • THE NATIONALS

Stacy and Sam are in Europe. Davy is at the Junior Championships in Kalamazoo. And it looks like Grandma is going to get married and move to Australia!

"What's happening to this family?" Betsy asked, and that's what I wanted to know, too.

Grandma'd met this old man at a Senior tournament in Las Vegas, and he seems kind of nice, but I don't like him. Why can't he come to live in Rock Canyon? "You said you had enough traveling," I told Grandma.

She'd changed her mind. She and Mr. Taylor are

acting just like Stacy and Sam did!

Stacy's sent us scenic postcards from a lot of different countries. Right now they're staying in a castle near a fantastic *wasserfall*. There was a picture of it on the card that came. "Austria is the most beautiful country of all," Stacy wrote. "I'm playing better, and I won some tournaments in France and Spain. Good luck to everybody at La Jolla."

We'd already had it.

"Sometimes there are advantages to having a small family," Mom told us. "How would you like to go on a trip?"

"Oh, boy!" Betsy said. "Where to?"

There was only one place I wanted to go, but I didn't say anything. It was too far.

"Mom and I managed to get our vacations at the same time," Dad said. "We could take the car and see something of the country."

My parents are always looking at road maps and planning trips that we never take. Dad has always been too busy with Stacy and Dave. So now they want to go on a trip, when all I want to do is to play tennis.

Mom spread out a big map on our dining room table. It was the whole United States. "Now, here we are," she said, pointing to San Diego County in the bottom left-hand corner. "We're on U.S. 80, right?"

U.S. 80 goes east from the Pacific Coast, right through Rock Canyon, and on up to the mountains and down into the desert on the other side. We've been there lots of times. But Dad put his finger on Highway 80 and traced it on across the Colorado River, through Arizona and New Mexico, to Texas. Then it went clear across Texas to . . . Louisiana!

"Louisiana!" I shrieked. "The National Girls' Fourteens!"

"Think you girls could get ready by Saturday?" Dad asked, and I shouted, "Oh, boy, could we!" I almost hugged the breath out of him, and Betsy was hugging Mom.

There *are* some advantages to having a small family. We each had a parent to ourself.

Dad got the car all fixed up on Friday, and we made plans to start at four A.M. Betsy and I woke up at two. We've never even been out of California!

Dad drove, and Mom had a book that told about the best places to eat and sleep and the interesting sights along the way.

The deserts I'd seen before were just dry, dirt flatlands or foothills, with sage and cactus and hardly any people or houses, only the highway stretching out for miles and miles. But just before we crossed the Colorado River into Yuma, Arizona, there was a beautiful white desert with drifty sand dunes.

"This is where they make Sahara Desert movies," Mom told us.

Mom kept figuring out interesting side trips we could take that would only be twenty or thirty miles

198

out of the way, but Dad said, "No. We can make Tucson this afternoon, and that'll give Dori a chance to practice on the university courts." That was fine with me. I'd rather play tennis than see sights.

The University of Arizona is a sight in itself. It has the most beautiful campus I've ever seen. After we checked in at a motel, Dad and I rallied on its courts. Mom and Betsy went shopping for souvenirs at an Indian Trading Post. Betsy got a turquoise bracelet for me.

The next day, we drove on through the lovely desert scenery of Arizona and New Mexico. All along the highway were reddish rock formations, carved into shapes like castles and fortresses. Betsy thought the Indians had done it, but Mom said that a long time ago, there had been deep rivers where we could only see dry gullies now, and that was what had made the rocks so beautiful.

That afternoon, we checked in at a motel in Las Cruces, New Mexico. It seemed like a million miles from nowhere, backed up against the purple Organ Mountains. After an early supper, we got our rackets and went to the university tennis courts. Dad wasn't taking any chances of me getting out of practice!

The next day, we drove on to Texas. I'd heard that Texas was a big state, but I didn't know how big till we drove across it, with purple mesas always in the distance on the flat, open ranges. We saw black Angus cattle, more sage and cactus, and an oil well

199

that had caught on fire and had black, billowing smoke and crimson flames going way up in the sky.

It kind of scared me, coming so far just to play in a tournament. "What if I don't win?" I asked. "What if I lose in the first round?"

"We're having fun, aren't we?" Mom said. "This is a very educational trip."

"Educational" is an unpleasant word, but I knew what she meant. "It's interesting to drive through the different states," I said. "I'd like to see the whole world, like Stacy."

"The best way to do that," Dad said, "is to be a tennis star."

So for *star*ters, I'd better win the National Girls' Fourteens.

The last day before we got to Louisiana, we stopped in Fort Worth. Betsy wanted to go to a rodeo (that's ro-DAY-oh), and Dad said okay. I've never seen so many horses in my life. Or cowboys! After we checked into our motel, Dad found a tennis court, a dirt one. "You ought to play all you can on clay," he told me.

Louisiana was a whole different world. After all those miles of dry desert country, it seemed like all the water in the world was in Louisiana. There were lakes and bayous (kind of soggy, marshy creeks, half water and half land) and the biggest river I've ever seen. Shreveport, where we stayed, is a big city, with skyscrapers and oil refineries on the bluffs over the Red River, where steamboats and barges pass by.

We checked into a motel, then drove to the tennis club where the Nationals were to be played. I was anxious to see the courts that Dad had told me about. There are all different kinds of clay, and these were sort of grayish green, more like packed, wet sand than the dusty-red dirt courts we'd practiced on along the way. And there were girls my age all over the place, hitting with each other on the courts, drinking pop in the clubhouse, comparing dresses and rackets and shoes, and yakking like they were at the world's biggest slumber party.

I didn't have to worry long about being left out. Three girls came over to me and said, "Hi! Where are you from?"

"California," I said. "I'm Dori Sinclair."

"This is Connie," the cutest one said. "She's from Michigan. I'm Teri, from Connecticut, and this is Caro-line, from Caro-lina."

"No'th Ca'lina," she said, with a friendly giggle.

They dragged me over to the draw, which was posted on a bulletin board. "If you're from California, you're probably seeded," Connie said. "*Are* you seeded?"

"I don't think so," I said, but I looked at the list. Luellen was number two, after a girl from Florida named Stephanie Hollis. There were eight seeds, and I was number six! In the *United States!* Wow!

"You get to play all year," Teri said. "That's a big help, especially in the Fourteens."

"How do they pick?" I asked.

"The officials from the different sections send in their rankings," Connie said. "And I suppose they have to do some guessing, since most of us from different parts of the country have never played each other."

"The other girl from California," Teri said, "Luellen Jarvis, played in the Nationals last year. Do you know her?"

"Yes," I said, and that was all I said. Let them find out!

I was glad that Luellen and I were on different sides of the draw. I wanted to beat her, but I wasn't in any hurry, especially if she'd had practice in the Nationals last year. There were sixty-four girls in the draw, and they came from all over: Florida, Pennsylvania, New York, Texas, Oregon, Minnesota, Puerto Rico, Washington, D.C., even Alaska and Hawaii.

"Now I know why it's worth coming all this way," I told Mom, "even if I don't win. It's interesting to meet all these girls."

But I wasn't planning on losing.

I didn't see Luellen that afternoon, and I was glad. All the girls I'd never known before were my friends already, and they invited me to hit with them. Thank goodness I had a chance to practice on those courts, because the tournament started the next day.

It was strange at first, hitting on that slow surface, but it wasn't too different. "You have more time to prepare your strokes," Connie told me, "and it's even more important to keep your eye on the ball." In Michigan, they get to play on hardcourts, clay, and even wood. Wood is the fastest; on hardcourts, you always get the same bounce; and clay feels better on your feet.

"On clay you get some funny bounces," Teri said, but Caroline told me that "girls from Califo'nia" who play on hardcourts all the time "jus' take to clay like a duck takes to watah." I loved the way she talked.

It was fun, but kind of warm, so I was sitting in the clubhouse drinking cold orange juice with a bunch of girls when Luellen showed up, about five o'clock. She and her dad had flown in from Los Angeles.

"I'm so glad you got to come, Dori," she told me. "If I'd only known, we could've played doubles together."

She was playing with Stephanie Hollis, the top seed, so I doubted that she was really disappointed. I sure wished Shelby could've come. I was fixed up with Melita Akina, a girl from Hawaii whom I hadn't even met yet. She wasn't seeded in the singles, so we probably wouldn't get very far. But, as Shelby would undoubtedly say, "If it weren't for us losers, there wouldn't be any tournaments.''

In the average local tournament, you can read the names on the draw and get a fair idea of how far you can go. But in this draw, I'd have to play top Four-teens from all over the country, one from a different state in every round!

The first day, I was lucky enough to get a steady player from Alabama, who gave me a lot of practice on the slow court. I won, 6–4, 6–0, and I learned how to slide! You can't slide on cement, unless it's slick from the rain, and then you have to quit playing unless you want to break your neck. But when you run on clay, you can sort of slide into your shots, and it sure is fun.

In the second round, I was afraid it was going to rain any minute—it sure rains a lot in Louisiana—and I got a bad case of The Elbow. I was playing a girl from New York who hit so hard that I couldn't get up to net, and we had long rallies that went on and on. I got impatient trying to finish up before the rain and lost the first set. That's when my arm turned into spaghetti.

I dashed around the court after every shot, and pushed it back, somehow. I was desperate, and I wished it *would* rain before I lost the match. At the start of every game I told myself, *You've got to win this one.* I'd only won one game, and the more I tried to win another, the worse I lost it, till it was my last chance. And she wasn't that good!

"The score is five games to one, second set," announced the umpire.

It was my serve, and I bounced the ball a few times, trying to think what to do. Then I remembered something Grandma had told me. "Five is a magic word," she'd said. "When you hear it, even if you're down five games in the second set, you can still win the match. Just take it one point at a time."

Forget about the rain, I told myself. *Forget about losing. Forget about everything except that ball!*

Boy, did I concentrate. When I came out of it, the umpire was announcing, "Game, set, and match to Dori Sinclair, four-six, seven-five, six-love.

And the sun was shining!

Dad was a wreck from all that suspense, and I found out that Luellen had been watching me, too, after she'd won her match, 6-0, 6-0.

"Congratulations, Dori," she said. "You really had me worried."

I bet.

On the third day, I won my singles, 6-3, 6-2, but Melita and I got knocked out of the doubles. I was afraid I had let her down, but she just laughed and invited me to Hawaii. "We'll beat everybody in the Islands," she told me.

The tournament officials must have been pretty good guessers, because we were down to the quarter finals with only eight players left, and every one was a seeded player!

MATCH POINT

We didn't play tennis all the time, of course. We had parties and boat rides and all kinds of fun. But I went to bed early the night before the quarters. I had to play Joyce Lee, a Chinese girl from San Francisco. She was seeded number three, so I was supposed to lose.

I knew any player from northern California would be tough, but I wasn't about to get psyched out. I just had to prove those seeders were wrong. And I did, 6-4, 7-5. I played my best, for a change.

The next day was the semis, and I was all charged up to beat the *top*-seeded player, Stephanie Hollis. I've never hit harder than I did in the first set, but Stephanie is a great retriever. She hits with both hands! I won the first set, 7-5, but I was exhausted.

It's a lot hotter in Louisiana than it is back home, but the weather hadn't been really bad till that day. It's a funny kind of heat, wet and steamy, and it drained my strength. I kept on hitting hard, but Stephanie kept getting them *all* back, so I tried following my serve to net. My legs felt like wet rags, and I didn't want to move, but I made myself.

"It's just as hot on the other side of the court," I muttered. But Stephanie is from Florida, so maybe she's used to that kind of weather. Anyway, she kept on getting my shots back, and getting them back, till she won the second set, 6-4.

All I wanted to do for our ten-minute break was sit down, but Dad said I should take a shower and put on some dry clothes. I took the shower; it was so steamy in there that I couldn't even get *myself* dry. But after a cool drink—no ice water, Dad had said—I went out again, ready for battle. Dad wouldn't tell me what to do, so I had to figure out something for myself. I guess he couldn't think of anything I hadn't *been* doing. But he gave me a big smile.

I concentrated on winning my serve, and didn't knock myself out to win hers, until the score was 5–4, my favor. Then I went all out. The score went to deuce, her ad, deuce, her ad, at least a hundred times. I wouldn't give up, and neither would she.

Then *finally, I* got an ad!

I didn't think about it. I just played tennis. She served short, figuring on drawing me in so that she could lob. *I* figured I'd just put my return away. I whaled it down the middle of the court, almost to the baseline. She managed to scoop it up somehow and highball it over my head. I ran back, but halfway there, a terrible pain knotted up the back of my leg, and I fell down on the court.

Cramps!

I knew what would happen next. They let you limp around and rub your leg for a minute, but that's all. I wouldn't be able to run, so I'd lose. Both my legs were knotting up, and they hurt so much that I couldn't help it: I sat there in the middle of the court, in front of all those people, and bawled.

207

But everybody was clapping, and the umpire was announcing, "Game, set, and match to Dori Sinclair, seven-five, four-six, six-four."

Then I found out what had happened. Stephanie's lob had gone out!

I got a telegram that night from Jimmy. "Congratulations," it said. "Just one more. We'll celebrate when you get back."

I felt okay the next day for the finals, but Dad decided I should take some salt tablets. I hadn't taken them before, because sometimes they make me sick to my stomach.

"We'll just have to risk that," Dad said. "It's another hot day."

Nobody had managed to upset Luellen, so there she was, waiting for *me*, for a change, on the championship court.

After I won the semis, Mom gave me a surprise—a pale green tennis dress that she'd brought along "for the finals."

"How'd you know I'd be in the finals?" I asked.

Mom just smiled and said, "It's lovely with your hair."

"You look as cool as a cucumber," Dad joked. The dress was the color of the inside of a cucumber, and it *was* real cool. It made me feel confident. For the first time, I thought I looked as nice as Luellen.

The stands were buzzing with all the best fourteen-year-olds in U.S. tennis, and I knew them all. They were my friends. They would always be my friends.

"Players ready? Linesitters ready? Play!" called the umpire.

The skies were clear, and there was a cool breeze from the lake. I felt so good that I couldn't miss anything. I won the first set, 6–0, and then I got to dreaming.

If you win a United States tennis championship, you get a little silver ball. Stacy has two, and maybe Davy was getting one back in Kalamazoo . . . and maybe. . . .

Luellen won her serve at the beginning of the second set, but I wasn't worried. I didn't expect to beat her, 0 and 0. Then the score went to deuce on my serve. That didn't bother me, either, but I sure woke up when Luellen got the ad.

I couldn't lose my serve.

I put in my best slice to her backhand and followed it to net, but Luellen hauled off and socked a down-the-line passing shot that whistled past my right ear.

"Game to Miss Jarvis," the umpire announced. "She leads, two games to love."

That service break followed me all the way to the end of the set. I couldn't break back, so she won the second set, 6–3.

So what if I'd won the first set, 6–0. We were dead even!

"For a little while there, I thought you had me," Luellen told me, when we left the court for our ten-minute rest. She chuckled as she walked away.

She was laughing. I wasn't.

In the third set, Luellen played better than I'd ever seen her play. I barely won my first serve after playing ad in, ad out, until the umpire started sounding hoarse. Then Luellen won her serve and broke mine, for 2–1; but I broke hers right back and won my own, for 3–2.

On her next service, Luellen hit her first two serves to my backhand, but I hit perfect returns, one to each corner, and she couldn't reach either of them. So what did she do? She hit *soft* serves to me that I socked out of bounds or into the net, so it was tied, at 3–3.

We both won our serves again, and it was 4–4, my serve coming up. If I won, then I'd just need to break her serve once more, and that little silver ball would be mine!

I served what I thought would be an ace to the far corner of her service court, but Luellen rushed over and smashed it low over the net. I lobbed it back to the same place, thinking she'd expect a crosscourt volley. But she got to it and drop-shot it where *I* had just been.

Love–15.

Then I double-faulted, and it was love–30! I wasn't thinking about little silver balls anymore!

After we volleyed my next serve a couple thousand times, I dinked! Luellen was so surprised that she dinked back, and I smashed it as hard as I could. The ball hit the top of the net and seemed to just balance there. Finally, it dribbled down the side of the net— on *her* side.

My next serve wasn't an ace, but it was good enough that all Luellen could do was chop it into the net. Then I did hit an ace, and it was 40–30.

I tried a twist serve to Luellen's backhand for the game point, but she lobbed it back to my backhand. We kept running each other across the court until I was ready to drop. Luellen still looked like a movie actor playing effortlessly. At last, somehow I turned a little extra at the last second and blazed the ball down the same sideline I was on. Luellen had automatically started for the other side of the court and couldn't get back in time.

Whew! Five games to four, my favor. Now all I had to do was break her serve!

But how?

Luellen went back to her soft serve. She'd been smart enough last time she'd served not to use it, so I hadn't figured it out yet. I just stood there, mesmerized, and watched it bounce by me. Then, all of a sudden, I realized what had gone wrong when I'd smashed it before: The clay surface had made it bounce just a little more straight up instead of toward the baseline. Teri had told me about the funny bounces, but they hadn't been so noticeable before. "Thanks, Teri," I muttered as I got ready to

211

receive Luellen's next serve.

Apparently thinking that I had The Elbow, Lu-ellen hit another soft serve and came up to net, but I hit a hard lob to her backhand that she didn't have a chance to reach. I guess she thought I'd just been lucky, because she tried it again, so I lobbed again, and it was 15–30!

Luellen's pretty smart, but she wasn't thinking very well then. She hit *another* soft serve and stayed back, expecting me to lob. I hit a perfect little drop shot that just cleared the net and died. Boy, was she mad!

I have to give her credit, though. She didn't panic. She went back to her hard serve and won the next point, for 30–40. If she caught up and won her serve, we'd be at 5–5 and maybe end up playing a tie breaker. I sure didn't want that!

The score did go to deuce, and we took turns get-ting the ad. One time when it was her ad, I scrambled so hard for a drop shot that I landed on my bottom in the middle of the service court. But I still got it back—sitting down.

The next time it was my ad, I scooped up a half-volley on my way to net, and spread my arms out and jumped back and forth to cover her return. She tried to pass me, but I outguessed her and was ready for her shot. I cut it off at the net with an angled overhead that just caught the edge of the ad-court sideline.

"Game, set, and match to Dori Sinclair!"

I wasn't dreaming. Betsy almost broke my neck, and Mom was crying. Girls from all over the United States were hugging me and inviting me to their homes.

Dad gave me a bear hug! Boy, did that feel good.

Suddenly I realized that Grandma and Mr. Taylor were there, too!

"We couldn't miss *this* match!" Grandma's fiancé said. Gol-lee! If I kept winning, maybe we'd see Grandma a lot, after all. And there are some pretty good tournaments in Australia, I guess.

"Is Australia on the way to Wimbledon?" I asked Grandma.

"It sure as glory *can* be," she said.

Gol-lee!

YOU WILL ENJOY

THE TRIXIE BELDEN SERIES
28 Exciting Titles

THE MEG MYSTERIES
6 Baffling Adventures

ALSO AVAILABLE

Algonquin
Alice in Wonderland
A Batch of the Best
More of the Best
Still More of the Best
Black Beauty
The Call of the Wild
Dr. Jekyll and Mr. Hyde
Frankenstein
Golden Prize
Gypsy from Nowhere
Gypsy and Nimblefoot
Lassie—Lost in the Snow
Lassie—The Mystery of Bristlecone Pine
Lassie—The Secret of the Smelters' Cave
Lassie—Trouble at Panter's Lake
Match Point
Seven Great Detective Stories
Sherlock Holmes
Shudders
Tales of Time and Space
Tee-Bo and the Persnickety Prowler
Tee-Bo in the Great Hort Hunt
That's Our Cleo
The War of the Worlds
The Wonderful Wizard of Oz